"This attrac
I..." Harris
can't happe

Frankie nodded. But her gaze stayed glued to his as if she knew the train was running off the track and was willing to risk full and complete disaster.

"Francesca..." The word was a final, husky plea for her to put some distance between them. She didn't. She moved toward him with an instinctive movement at the same time he brought her closer with a palm to the bare skin of her back. It felt even sexier than he remembered.

His fingers curved around her delicate jaw, and for the first time in as long as he could remember, he did something for the pure pleasure of it. He kissed the woman he'd been wanting to touch since the night he'd found her sitting in his former assistant's chair.

Her lush mouth was every bit as sweet as it had promised it would be. A soft sigh left her lips as she moved into the kiss, her hands fluttering to his shoulders. The dominant male in him liked her acquiescence.

His body temperature spiked. He didn't know the last time he'd felt so...*lost*.

Her innocence should have stopped him. Instead it obliterated his common sense.

The Tenacious Tycoons

Two billionaire brothers to be reckoned with!

Brothers Harrison and Coburn, heirs to the great
American Grant dynasty, have everything they
could desire—the money, the power and the
tenacity to take whatever they want. Yet money
can't buy everything, and if these brothers hope to
live up to their family legacy they'll each need
a very special woman by their side.

But the rules of love are nothing like that of
business—and when it comes to the
game of passion, securing the deal is
never as easy as it first seems...

Read Harrison's story in
TEMPTED BY HER BILLIONAIRE BOSS
June 2015

And read Coburn's story,
coming October 2015

Jennifer Hayward

———

Tempted by Her Billionaire Boss

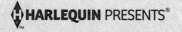
HARLEQUIN PRESENTS®

ISBN-13: 978-0-373-13348-2

Tempted by Her Billionaire Boss

First North American publication 2015

Recycling programs
for this product may
not exist in your area.

Printed in U.S.A.

TM www.Harlequin.com

Jennifer Hayward has been a fan of romance since filching her sister's novels to escape her teenage angst. Her career in journalism and PR, including years of working alongside powerful, charismatic CEOs and traveling the world, has provided perfect fodder for the fast-paced, sexy stories she likes to write, always with a touch of humor. A native of Canada's east coast, Jennifer lives in Toronto with her Viking husband and young Viking-in-training.

Books by Jennifer Hayward

Harlequin Presents

The Magnate's Manifesto
Changing Constantinou's Game

Society Weddings
The Italian's Deal for I Do

The Delicious De Campos
The Divorce Party
An Exquisite Challenge
The Truth About De Campo

Visit the Author Profile page
at Harlequin.com for more titles.

For Michelle. You've been a rock
and an inspiration for me right from the beginning.
Thank you for being you.

CHAPTER ONE

ROCKY BALBOA PATROLLED the length of his rectangular glass-encased world with an increasingly agitated fervor, the blinding beam of the overhead fluorescent lights a far from suitable atmosphere for Frankie Masseria's high-strung orange parrot cichlid fish. Used to the cozy confines of Coburn Grant's muted, stylish office with its custom lighting and plentiful dimmers, Rocky apparently wasn't making the transition to Harrison Grant III's cold black-and-chrome domain any more easily than Frankie herself was.

Her mouth twisted in a grimace. She would make the poor joke of being a fish out of water in this startling new development of her as the replacement PA for the CEO of Grant Industries if her stomach wasn't dipping and turning along with Rocky's distressed flips and circles. Harrison Grant, the elder of the two Grant brothers from Long Island, heirs to an automotive fortune, was notorious for his ability to go through a PA a quarter until her predecessor Tessa Francis had taken over two years ago and tamed the legendary beast. Known for her formidable attitude and ability to whip any living thing into line, including even the snooty, tyrannical Harrison Grant, Tessa would have continued to keep the world a safer place for everybody had she not elected to do the very human thing of getting pregnant and requesting a six-month maternity leave. A reasonable request in many parts of the world, but not in the frantic, pulsing-with-forward-momentum world of Manhattan. Frankie had heard of female CEOs texting from the labor room. Yelling orders in between pushes. Not that that would ever be *her*. When she eventually found the perfect man to settle down with, she'd put raising her children first, unlike her parents who'd had them working in the Masseria family restaurant as soon as they were old enough to bus a table.

But that was then and this was now. She sighed and looked down at the massive amount of work sitting on her desk, unsure of what to tackle next. This wouldn't be *her* mess to weed through had Tessa orchestrated the orderly exit she'd been intent on and found a new PA for her impossible boss. But, according to Tessa, Harrison had simply *refused* to acknowledge she was leaving. His eyes would glaze over at the subject every time she brought it up, until finally, with time running out, Tessa had gone ahead and scheduled the interviews.

That's when the unthinkable had happened. Tessa had gone into premature labor last night while Harrison was on a business trip to Hong Kong, the interviews had been canceled and Frankie had been installed in her place by her magnanimous boss Coburn, who had decided his brother could not be without a PA. Without so much as a "would you mind, Frankie?"

"It's the perfect opportunity to shine," he'd told her in that cajoling voice of his. "Six months with Harrison and you'll be back with a whole new visibility within the company."

Or she would be just another piece of Harrison Grant's road kill, Frankie thought miserably. It had been her dream as long as she'd been old enough to apply eye shadow and visited her friend Olga's father in his swanky Manhattan office, to be a glamorous PA. To wear beautiful suits to the office every day, to live in the vibrant city she loved and to work in the upper echelons of power where all the big deals were made.

If that had gone against her parents' wishes to have her remain in the family restaurant business, so be it. She'd put herself through administrative-assistant school with her tip money, graduated top of her class and gone after her dream.

Landing a job with the insanely handsome, charming younger Grant brother, Coburn, had seemed like her dream come true. Working for the legendary Grant family, who commanded one of America's oldest automotive dynasties from one of Manhattan's marquee skyscrapers, was like taking her "what do I want to be in five years" plan and fast-forwarding it *five years*.

She had seized the opportunity with both hands, molding herself into the epitome of efficiency and professionalism in her six months with Coburn. Her boss's flashing blue eyes and easy smile wore his vice presidency with a stark sex appeal few women could resist, but resist Frankie had. She knew he'd hired her for both her skills and the fact she hadn't fallen all over him in the interview like the others had. In return, he'd been a dream to work with. He appreciated every ounce of the tightly coiled efficiency she brought to his office, reining in his tendency to run askew with his passion for his work.

So why throw her to the wolves so easily? She swallowed past the distressed lump in her throat and took a sip of the herbal French lavender tea that was *supposed* to calm her. Harrison Grant was reputed to be as serious and tunnel-visioned as his younger brother was hot-blooded and impulsive. He had a filthy temper from all accounts. She said "from all accounts" because Tessa had always shielded her from her boss, coming downstairs to

Coburn's office if she needed something rather than expose Frankie to one of his moods. Frankie had accepted the arrangement gladly. She could live without having to deal with the massive ego of the man voted most likely to become president by his peers at Yale, his alma mater. Rumor had it that time wasn't far off for the thirty-three-year-old Harrison. Her father had told her he had enough clout within the business community to run as an independent in the next election and, in these disaffected times, he just might win.

If that happened, Coburn would take over as CEO and Frankie would be head honcho admin. The perfect career scenario by all accounts. *If* she survived the next six months.

A throb pulsed its way from her left temple through to the center of her head as she considered the files Tessa had left marked urgent. A key takeover to help facilitate, shareholder meetings to organize, a trip to India coming up in just weeks... It seemed way beyond her means.

Rocky caught her attention out of the corner of her eye, swimming now in faster, demonic circles as if signaling an imminent disaster. His eyes bulged out of his aristocratic head, his expression foreboding. *Yes, I know*, Frankie wanted to reassure him, *but we have twenty-four hours to prepare for his arrival.*

Which meant she needed to get this work done. Despite her misgivings about the whirlwind change in plans, she was determined to prove to Harrison Grant she was the best PA he could ever have behind Tessa, a modern-day version of Wonder Woman. There was no other possible outcome.

The acquisition file was on top of the heap. Apparently Grant Industries was in the midst of attempting to purchase Siberius, a Russian automotive parts supplier. Job number one, Tessa had managed to tell her on the way to the hospital, was to finish the additional background Harrison had requested to support two outstanding contract negotiation points.

She scanned it, decided it was going to be a long night and rifled around in Tessa's desk until she found some takeout menus. The local Thai place appealed. She ordered herself some dinner to be delivered, slipped off her shoes and got comfortable. At seven, the new security guard brought her food up, noticed she was working alone and said he'd check on her throughout the evening. Deciding Harrison Grant owed her a glass of Pinot Grigio for this one, she procured a bottle of reasonably, but not overly, expensive wine from the heftily stocked bar in his office, took it back to her desk with a glass and opened it.

She was about to dig into her noodles when she realized the restaurant had forgotten to include a fork in the bag. Eating noodles with her hands not being an option, she toed her way around for her shoes and came up empty. She stuck her head under the massive desk and looked for them. It was dark under there and it took her eyes a few moments to adjust. Finally she located a shoe she'd kicked to the left and was holding it triumphantly in her hand and reaching for the second when a deep voice laced with an arctic coolness pierced the solid wooden desk.

"It didn't occur to me you were going to like it, Geoffrey. I pay people like you to make things happen, not for your incredibly insightful strategic thinking."

Harrison Grant. Oh, my God. What is he doing back tonight?

She reared her head up, her skull connecting hard with the inch-thick top of the desk. Stars exploded behind her eyes. A curse escaped her as she dropped the shoe, clasped her head in her hands and absorbed the pulsing aftershocks.

"Good God." The harsh-edged voice came closer. "Geoffrey, I'm going to have to call you back."

Frankie was vaguely aware of strong male hands levering her chair away from the desk and lifting her chin. She blinked as he pulled her hands from her head, and tipped her skull back. A clear head might have been a good weapon to face Harrison Grant with for the first time, but her cerebral matter was hazy, her vision shadowy as she took him in at close range. Dressed in a black trench coat in deference to the rainy, overcast New York day, he was tall, imposingly tall. The charcoal-gray suit he wore beneath the trench coat, the amount of rough stubble shading his aristocratic jaw and the laser-like stare of his black eyes under designer glasses made her giddily wonder if he was the devil himself.

Biting out a low curse, he tossed his cell phone on the desk and cupped the back of her head with one of his big hands, his fingers pressing into her scalp to feel for a bump. When he located the growing mass that was causing the deep throb in her head, a furrow ruffled his brow. "What exactly were you doing down there?"

"Shoes," Frankie muttered absently as the world began to right itself. She sucked in a couple of deep breaths and examined him closer. Along with those deadly dark eyes, he had a perfect aquiline nose that framed a firm, wide mouth. Apparently the devil came in extremely good-looking versions that also smelled amazing.

He held up three fingers. "How many?"

"Three."

"What day is it?"

"Tuesday, the sixth of August."

He let his fingers slide from her head. His black gaze, however, remained pinned on her face. "Unless this is *Goldilocks and the Three Bears* redone to feature a brunette, *you* are sitting in the wrong chair."

Her heart sped up in her chest at his low, silky tone, as curiosity radiated from the inky darkness of his somewhat mesmerizing gaze. "What if this is actually the *right* chair?" she offered in an attempt to defuse the tension.

His mouth curved. "Now I know that would have to be a tale, because this chair belongs to my assistant, Tessa, and *you*," he murmured, his sweeping stare taking in all of her, including a rather comprehensive study of her legs, "are not her."

Frankie swallowed hard and followed his gaze. In the commotion, her conservative skirt had ridden up her thighs, baring the lacy black pull-ups that were her one nod toward femininity in her proper office attire. *Oh, God.* She tugged the summer-weight wool back to her knees, so much heat rushing to her face she might as well have been on fire. With difficulty, she moved her gaze back up to his and saw...*disappointment*?

"Tessa," she murmured, searching vainly for a way to rescue the situation, "went into premature labor and had her baby last night. Co—" Her words died in her throat as a flash of silver glinted across the room. She blinked, thinking her swimming head had manufactured it, but when she looked again, the sight of two armed guards bearing down on them, guns drawn, made her mouth drop open.

"Put your hands in the air."

The guards roared the words at them, their attention fixed on Harrison. Frankie stuck her hands in the air, her heart slamming so violently against her chest she thought she might pass out. Her gaze sat frozen on the glare of the lights reflected off the silver barrels.

She tore her panicked gaze away finally, flicking it to Harrison, whose face had a bemused look on it. Instead of following the guard's orders, he put his palms on his thighs and moved to straighten.

"I said put your hands in the air," the guard bellowed, waving his gun at Harrison. *"Now."*

Her boss put his suit-clad arms in the air in a slow, exaggerated movement. He might have acquiesced, but every muscle in his big body was tensed to revolt, his black gaze glittering. They sensed it, their eyes remaining trained on him. "Hands behind your back."

The CEO's mouth parted. "I think—"

"Hands behind your back."

Her boss put his hands behind his back, a dark thundercloud stealing over his face. The guard closest to him holstered his gun, turned the CEO around with a careful appreciation of his powerful frame and snapped handcuffs around his wrists.

Oh, my God. Frankie's frozen brain registered the guards now as Grant Industries security guards. But what were they doing arresting Harrison Grant?

The guard with his gun still drawn crooked a finger at Frankie. "Over here."

The logical part of her brain told her she didn't want anything to do with a man with a gun. Even one in uniform. Maybe these men were *posing* as Grant security guards. Maybe they wanted to *rob* them…

"Move," the guard growled at her. Frankie's behind left the chair in a hurry. She wasn't sure how she did it because her legs were mush, but she wobbled over to where the guard stood, shaking so hard her teeth chattered. His partner pushed Harrison down in the chair she'd vacated.

"What happened?" the guard beside Frankie asked.

She gave him an uncomprehending look. 'Wh-what do you mean? You just came tearing in here…"

"You hit the panic button."

Panic button. What panic button? She vaguely remembered something in her training about an emergency button she could press if anything ever happened, but she'd laughed it off at the time, thinking it would be more useful for handling Coburn's discarded girlfriends than an actual *situation*. Hers had been on the wall beside her desk.

Her gaze slid to the wall beside Tessa's desk. No button.

"It's under the desk on the left," the guard said.

Under the desk? Her gaze slid to the big mahogany desk where her new boss sat *handcuffed.* A sick feeling enveloped her. She must have hit the button by mistake when Harrison walked in and startled her.

Oh, good lord.

The guard pointed at Harrison. "Pete said you were up here working alone. *He* had his hands on you when we arrived."

Frankie's stomach rolled. The guards were new. They'd changed to a different company last week. "*He,*" she clarified weakly, "is Harrison Grant, the CEO of this company. I hit the panic button by mistake."

The guards assumed identical gray complexions. Harrison Grant's expression moved from one of disbelief to an even darker countenance Frankie chose to avoid.

The guard beside her turned and surveyed the tall, elegant male in the chair dubiously. "You're supposed to be abroad."

Harrison's dark-as-night eyes glittered back at him. "I parked underground and took the back elevators."

"You don't look like your picture."

Frankie wanted to scream not to poke the beast. The glimmer in the CEO's eyes turned deadly. "I can assure you that she," he said, nodding his head at Frankie, "whoever she is, is telling the truth. Being the workaholic I am, I've acquired glasses since my last headshot."

"You got some ID?"

Her boss dipped his chin. "Front pocket."

The guard closest to Harrison retrieved his wallet from his jacket with a ginger movement that made Frankie hysterically wonder what he thought he'd do. *Bite him?* The man had his hands manacled behind his back. The guard flipped the wallet open, scanned it and went even grayer. Bile climbed the back of Frankie's throat.

"Apologies for the confusion." The guard slid the wallet back into Harrison's pocket. "The situation you two were in, the bottle of wine, we read it wrong."

Frankie's gaze flew to the bottle of Pinot Grigio on the desk. *Oh, heavens.* The way Harrison had been leaning over her... They couldn't possibly have thought this had been an assignation gone wrong...could they?

The grim look on her boss's face suggested that's exactly what they'd thought. He directed a laser-like stare at the guard. "You have exactly five seconds to get these cuffs off me."

The guard retrieved his key and had Harrison stand and turn around while he removed the cuffs. "We work on rotation," he said apologetically as he slid them off. "We're new in this building. So sorry we didn't recognize you, Mr. Grant."

Her boss extended his arms and flexed his wrists to get the circulation going. "Well, now that we've established we're all new, except *me*," he drawled, planting his gaze on Frankie, "and we've also determined this was *not* a romantic encounter with a bad ending for the sake of the gossip mill, perhaps you can tell me who *you* are, Goldilocks not being a suitable answer."

She bit down hard on her lip. "Francesca Masseria. Your brother's PA. Actually...yours now."

"Is that so?" Frankie watched her career hang in the balance of that dark, unfathomable gaze. It occurred to her she'd be lucky to get shipped back to Coburn.

The CEO turned his attention to the guards. "I suggest you start taking some regular walks around the building to learn who people are."

The guards nodded in unison. "Absolutely, sir."

Harrison waved a hand at them. "Go."

Frankie stood quaking in the center of the suddenly silent foyer as the silver-uniformed security detail disappeared toward the elevators. Her boss stood, legs planted wide in front of her, a distinct smoky gray aura surrounding his muscular frame.

She liked him better in handcuffs.

Harrison's mouth curled in a mocking smile. "Despite what you may have heard otherwise, Ms. Masseria, I am not a monster."

The rebuke stung her into silence. "I'm to assume," he drawled, "that you are filling in as Tessa's replacement until we can find someone else?"

"Actually Coburn has asked me to work with you until Tessa comes back."

His gaze narrowed on her speculatively. "Coburn thinks the sun rises and sets with your appearance in the office every morning, Ms. Masseria. How could we possibly expect him to get along without you for six months?"

Warmth stung her cheeks at the unexpected compliment. "I'm sure he'll manage," she demurred. "Nobody's irreplaceable."

"Tessa is."

She flinched. He considered her for a moment, his unnervingly precise gaze seeming to take a visual X-ray of her for further examination. "I need some sleep," he concluded. "Take your dinner and the wine, go home, get some rest and we'll talk about this in the morning."

Frankie took a step toward him. "I have some—"

He lifted a hand. "I have just flown sixteen hours to get home to be told my brilliant right hand and irreplaceable PA is in the hospital having a baby while in the midst of helping me with a crucial acquisition. I've been put in handcuffs by my own security team and had guns pointed at my face. And if that isn't enough, my body is heavily protesting the jump in time zones. The only thing," he underscored harshly, "that is going to make me feel like a human being at this point in time is a good stiff drink and a horizontal position on a bed that is my own. And *you*, Ms. Masseria, are the only thing standing between me and it. So unless you would like to finish this conversation *there*, put your shoes on and let's call it a night."

Her mouth fell open. Had he actually just said that? And why did she find that idea vastly exciting instead of incredibly inappropriate?

His eyes widened imperceptibly, then narrowed. "Joking, Ms. Masseria. Go home."

She looked down at her bare feet on the marble, her muted pink toenails the ultimate in complete humiliation. *Never* in the six months she had worked for Coburn had she ever acted this unprofessional.

But, she told herself lifting her chin, the first step toward redemption was moving on. They would come back in the morning as he'd said, she would show him what she was made of and it would all be fine.

"I will see you in the morning, then. We'll go through the urgent items then."

He inclined his head. She turned and headed toward her desk. Harrison's deep baritone halted her. "Ms. Masseria?"

She turned around.

"Which hospital is Tessa in?"

"Mount Sinai."

The humor that flickered in his eyes then caught her off guard. It made him look almost *human.* "Do you think you can send her some flowers from me in the morning without calling in the cavalry?"

She pressed her lips together. "I'll have it taken care of."

The beast was safely ensconced in his office repacking his briefcase when she ducked her head in to say she was leaving. He wished her an absentminded good-night and told her to take a taxi. Exhausted, she did. When she got home she swallowed down two painkillers for her throbbing head, reheated and ate half the noodles, then immersed herself in a hot bath.

She had just laid her head on the pillow when her cell phone rang. She frowned and pulled it off the bedside table. *Unknown caller.* She was about to decline the call when the thought they'd call back and wake her up made her reach for it.

"Francesca," she murmured sleepily into the phone.

"Just checking that whack on your head didn't do you in."

Harrison Grant's deep voice sent her jackknifing upright. How the heck did he have her mobile number? *The company directory.* Right.

"I was concerned about you. I should have sent you to the hospital to have your head looked at."

"I'm fine," she croaked. Without that arctic chill in it, his voice was the sexiest thing she'd ever heard over a phone line—deep, velvety and laced with a husky fatigue that reached all the way to her nerve endings.

Hadn't he been about to go to bed? *Was he calling from bed?*

She shook her head, wincing as the throbbing reminded her she shouldn't do that. How could she possibly be experiencing erotic images of a man who would likely send her packing tomorrow?

"Do you live with anyone?"

She blinked. "I—I don't think that's the kind of question I have to answer, is it?"

The warm, very masculine laughter that reached her from the other end of the line made the hairs on the back of her neck stand up. "I wasn't inquiring about your dating life, Francesca. I was going to say if you do have a roommate or significant other, you should get them to wake you up every few hours to make sure you don't have a concussion. They can be very serious."

"Oh." Frankie swallowed back a fresh wave of mortification. "That's very thoughtful of you. I do—have a roommate—that is. She's out but I'll do that."

"Good. See you in the morning, then."

She muttered good-night and disconnected the call. Punching down her pillow, she welcomed the breeze that wafted in through her old Victorian window, cooling her heated cheeks. Harrison Grant could add *ridiculously naive* to his new PA's description after tonight's debacle. That was, if he chose to keep her... She wasn't laying odds on it.

CHAPTER TWO

HARRISON'S MOUTH WAS DRY—parched with anticipation. His entire body was rigid with the expectation of physical satisfaction as the beautiful brunette rose from his office chair and pushed him down into it. Her soft, lush thighs hitting his as she straddled him made his heart catch in his throat. The lacy black stockings she wore with garters made an appearance, sending his blood coursing through his veins. *He had to have her. Now.*

Her long, silky dark hair brushed his face as she bent and kissed him. His hands reached blindly for the lace on her thighs, needing to touch. She slapped his fingers away. "Wait," she instructed in a husky, incredibly sexy voice. "Not yet."

He started to protest, but she pressed her fingers to his lips, reached behind her and pulled out something metal that glinted in the dim light of the desk lamp. *Handcuffs. Mother of God.*

He jackknifed to a sitting position. Sweat dripped from his body. Reality slapped him in the face as he discovered he wasn't being seduced in his office chair by a stunning brunette; he was in his own bed. Stunning disappointment followed. His racing heart *wanted* her. His body was pulsing, crying out for her to finish what she'd started…

An appalled feeling spread through him. He only knew

one set of eyes that particular shade of gray. *His new PA. He had been fantasizing about his new PA.*

A harsh curse left his mouth. He swung his legs over the side of the bed and brought his breathing under control. His dream had been wholly inappropriate. Never had he brought sex into the office and never would he. The guns and the handcuffs had truly pushed him over the edge.

And the stockings. That might actually have been the worst.

The birds were already singing. He poured himself into the shower and attempted to clear his head. The dull throb in his temple he'd been harboring for days was still there, reminding him normal human beings needed at least six hours of sleep on a regular basis to function at optimal performance.

His mouth twisted. Not that anyone considered him a normal human being. They thought he was a machine.

He toweled himself off, put his aching body in front of a cup of coffee and the newspaper and tried to focus on the rather mundane headlines. But his utterly incongruous dream kept working its way into his head.

He never had fantasies like that. He identified his urges, satisfied them according to a convenient slot in his insane schedule with a woman who didn't mind his lack of commitment, then he filed them back where they belonged: extracurricular activity that came after work.

His coffee cup went *thump* on the breakfast table. There was no way he could have *that* woman working for him. He took a last gulp of coffee, tossed the paper aside and headed for the gym in his building. He'd talk to Coburn when he got in. Tell him this just wasn't going to work.

Coburn strolled into his office a few minutes after he'd landed there, looking disgustingly fresh and sharp in a navy blue Armani suit. That they were both early risers who appreciated the benefits of physical exercise was about their only similarity. Even their intent in doing it was different. Harrison slotted it into his schedule like any other appointment, because if he didn't he'd be regularly seeing a heart specialist somewhere around fifty. It was in the Grant family genes.

Coburn, on the other hand, pursued mad daredevil-type sports that skirted death on a regular basis. Paragliding, mountain climbing, bicycle racing in European countries with tiny alpine ledges for tracks. Not to mention what it did for his physique, which maintained the steady flow of females in and out of his life so there would never be a dearth where he'd have to consider what the hell he was actually doing. His ex-wife had messed him up and messed him up good. But since that topic had long been considered subject *non grata*, Harrison began with the topic of the hour.

"How selfless of you to loan me Francesca Masseria." He sat back in his desk chair and took his Kenyan brew with him.

"Isn't it?" Coburn grinned. He took the seat opposite him. "Sometimes I can sacrifice for the greater good, H."

Harrison frowned. He hated when Coburn called him H and he knew it. "How many times have you slept with her?"

His brother gave him a look of mock offence. "Not even once. Although it's tempting. If God designed the perfect woman and set her down on this earth, it'd be Frankie and those legs of hers."

"Francesca," Harrison corrected, refusing to go there. "And you don't speak about an employee in that manner."

You just had hot, explicit dreams about them.

Coburn rolled his eyes.

"You've moaned about not having a good PA for years, then when you get one you love, you hand her over to me. *Why?*"

His brother trained his striking blue gaze on him the way he did the board when he wanted them on their knees. "Self-preservation. Frankie is a knockout. Of late, I've discovered she has a crush on me, although not one of her very proper bones would ever admit it. It's only a matter of time before we end up in bed together and I want to *prevent* that from happening because I want to *keep* her as my PA." He shrugged. "So I send her to the school of Harrison for six months, you train her with that regimental authority of yours, and I get her back when I am fully immersed in someone else, better than she was before."

If Harrison hadn't known his younger brother as well as he did, he would have assumed he was joking. But this was Coburn, who possessed every genetic trait the youngest born was created to feature, including an exaggerated sense of the need for his own independence from everything, including serious relationships with females and his responsibilities to Grant Industries.

"You do realize if HR heard even a quarter of that speech, I'd have to fire you."

Coburn lifted a Rolex-clad hand. "Then I retire to the south of Italy, road-race most of the year and manage my shares from there. Either works for me."

Harrison tamped down the barely restrained aggression he felt toward his younger brother. "She's not experienced enough for the job."

"This is Frankie we're talking about. You'll see when you meet her."

"Francesca," Harrison corrected again. "And I met her last night."

Coburn frowned. "How? You've only just gotten back."

"She was working late. Likely trying to make sense of things with Tessa's abrupt departure… I stopped in for a file."

"Your own fault," Coburn pointed out. "You've known for months Tessa was leaving and you did nothing about it."

Because he couldn't bear to be without his mind-bogglingly good PA who made his insane life bearable. Avoidance had been preferable...

"Anyway," Coburn continued, "it's the perfect solution for both of us. Frankie is incredible. Green, yes, but just as smart as Tessa. And," he added, pausing for effect, "she speaks Russian."

"Russian?"

"Fluently. Plus Italian, but I'm thinking the Russian is going to be more useful to you right now."

"How does she speak Russian?"

Coburn frowned. "I think she said her best friend is Russian. Something like that..."

Given his solitary goal in life at the moment was to obliterate Anton Markovic, the man who'd put his father in his grave, and negotiations to make it happen were at an extremely fragile stage with Leonid Aristov balking at the deal to acquire his company, a PA who could speak Russian could be a very valuable asset.

The amusement faded from Coburn's face. "You don't have to keep at this, you know? Father is ten feet under. He's never going to see you bring Markovic down. You're doing this for *you*, Harrison, not him. And lord knows you need a life."

His hands curled tightly around his coffee mug, his knuckles gleaming white. His younger brother's lack of interest in avenging the man who had built this company was a position he had long understood. His personal opinions on how *he* lived his life? Meaningless, when he had always been the only person holding this company together.

He put his coffee cup down on the desk before he crushed it between his fingers, and focused his gaze on his brother. "How about you keep playing with those in-

ternational markets and making us money like you do and
save your philosophical sermons for someone who cares?"

Coburn's easygoing expression slid into one approach-
ing the frigidness of his. "Someday you're going to realize that cold heart of yours has left you alone in this big
empty world, H. And when you do, nobody is going to
care anymore. But that's okay, because you will have your
vengeance."

Harrison flashed him a "see yourself out" look. Coburn
stood, straightened his suit coat and paused by the door.
"I gave you Frankie because you need her. But if you so
much as cause one tear to roll down her face, you'll answer to me for it. You hear me?"

His brother disappeared in a wave of expensive aftershave. Harrison glanced at the clock on the wall. Seven-
thirty. It was 7:30 a.m. and already he was exhausted. His
life exhausted him.

Frankie came to work armed and ready, although that
might be an unfortunate turn of phrase given last night's
occurrences. "Okay," she admitted to Rocky, who still
looked less than thrilled to be in his new surroundings,
but marginally calmer than yesterday, "let's just say that
was a bad choice of words."

She had worn her most expensive suit today, which
wasn't very expensive given her limited budget for a ward-
robe after paying rent for the brownstone apartment she
shared with Josephine. But she'd altered it so it looked
custom, the lightweight, charcoal-gray tailored jacket and
skirt hugging her curves without broadcasting the depth
of them. The color did something for her dark hair and
gray eyes she considered inferior to those of her striking
female siblings, and her chignon, well, it was the most
perfect she'd ever attempted. Geri from Accounting had
looked noticeably envious this morning on the elevator,

and if there was a morning she needed to win their dueling hairstyle competition, it was this.

She needed all the confidence she could muster facing her new boss this morning. *If* he decided to keep her.

Dumping her purse in her drawer, she ignored her rumbling stomach. She'd tried to eat, but she hadn't been able to get any breakfast down except a slice of toast and juice. She refused to call it nerves because she needed to have full armor on this morning. She'd been noticeably jumpy when the security guard had checked her ID downstairs and that scene of her boss in handcuffs kept replaying itself over and over in her head.

And then there had been his bedroom voice last night on the phone and her resulting descent into lunacy… Her stomach dipped. Today she was going to revert back to her usual, capable self: five steps ahead of her boss at all times, unruffleable and cheerful no matter what the request. And she was going to stay far, far away from that panic button. In fact, she was going to cover it with tape.

Mouth set in a firm gesture of determination, she ran her hands over her head to ensure every hair was in place and, satisfied she was all cool sophistication, walked toward Harrison's office. His brisk, clipped voice directing a conference call stopped her in her tracks. This was good. It would give her time to get organized. Having a boss who came in at 7:00 a.m. left you a bit flat-footed.

She made herself a cup of tea and scanned her email. Tessa had evaded her husband's watchful eye long enough to send her some notes from her smartphone. Frankie sank back in her seat, took a sip of her tea and ploughed gratefully through her list of Harrison rules.

Triage his email first thing in the morning and keep an eye on anything urgent. He's married to his smart-

phone, but the volume is overwhelming. You might
have to jump in.

Take his phone messages on the pink message pad
on the desk, not the blue one, and don't write on the
second half of the page. He likes to make notes for
follow-up there.

Fail on that one. She'd put a stack of messages on Harrison's desk last night that had used the whole page. She'd
fix that today…

Don't ever put a call through to him from any
woman other than a business contact or his mother.
Casual dates like to pose as girlfriends when they're
not. He hasn't had a regular woman in his life for a
while. Apparently, as you likely know from the gossip pages, he's supposed to be marrying Cecily Hargrove to cement the family dynasty, but I have seen
no evidence of her of late, so proceed with caution
and never talk with the press.

Fascinating. She was nothing if not discreet.

If he asks you to send flowers to a woman, send
calla lilies. They're his go-to choice. If he ever asks
you to send anything else, you can bet she's "the
one."

Frankie smiled. Although she couldn't imagine Harrison Grant ever falling for a woman like that.

Somewhere between eight and nine he will call
you into his office to put together a to-do list for the
day. Execute the list in the order he gives it to you.
He's like the Swiss train system. He needs things

done in a certain way at a certain time. Stick to this
and you'll be fine.

Wow. He was even more of a control freak than she was.

And, finally, don't ever interrupt him when he's
on a conference call. Put a note in front of him if
you have to. But since he spends four or five hours
on them a day, do bring him coffee. The Kenyan
blend—black. He figures out lunch himself.

Ugh. She glanced toward Harrison's office. She hadn't
done that. That necessitated facing him.

Getting to her feet, she brewed a steaming cup of Kenyan blend in the kitchen, slipped into Harrison's office
with the stealth of a cat and headed toward his desk. He
was on speakerphone, pacing in front of the windows like
a lethal weapon as he talked. She had almost made it to
the desk when he turned around.

Her nerves, the intensity of his black stare and the depth
of his intimidating good looks in the pinstriped three-piece
suit he wore like billionaire armor set her hand to shaking.
Hard. Coffee sloshed over the side of the mug and singed
her hand. Fire raced along the tender skin between her
thumb and forefinger. She bit back a howl of pain, set the
mug on the desk, speed walked to the outer office and put
it under cold water in the kitchen.

A couple of minutes under the tap made the burn bearable. She spread some salve from the emergency kit on
it and retraced her steps into Harrison's office where he
was still spewing point after point into the speakerphone.
Her gaze locked on the precious dark wood of the desk.
A large water ring stared back at her, embedded into the
wood. *Oh, no. Please, no.*

She scrubbed at it to no avail. Moved the mug to a

coaster and retreated to her desk. Sat there mentally calculating how long it would take him to fire her. Five more minutes on the conference call, a couple of minutes to think of how he was going to do it and *bam*—she'd be gone.

"Get ready to move again," she told Rocky.

Coward, his elegant snout accused.

"You try dealing with tall, dark and dangerous. Heavy on the dangerous."

Footsteps on the marble brought her head up. Dangerous had emerged from his office and conference call, three minutes early. He was looking at her as if she was quite possibly mad. "Who are you talking to?"

Frankie waved her hand at Rocky. "Rocky Balboa, meet Harrison Grant."

A dark brow lifted. "Rocky Balboa as in the boxer, Rocky?"

She nodded, heat filling her cheeks.

"You talk to a fish?"

"That is true, yes."

There was a profound silence. Frankie closed her eyes and waited for the two words to come. *You're fired.*

"Give me your hand."

She opened her eyes. He was looking at her burnt hand. "It's fine," she refused, tucking it under the desk. "I'm so sorry about the coffee stain. I'll see if the cleaners can work some magic."

"It can be sanded and refinished."

At an *insane* cost. Why was he being so reasonable about it? She swallowed hard. "Do you want to go through the priorities for today?"

"No, I want to see your hand. *Now*."

She stuck it out. He took it in his and ran the pad of his thumb over her fire-engine-red knuckles. Frankie's stomach did a slow roll at the innocent contact. It didn't seem innocent coming from her fire-breathing boss. It seemed—disturbing.

He sighed. "If we're going to be able to work together, you have to stop being afraid of me."

Gray eyes met black. He *wanted* her to keep working for him?

"I'm not afraid of you."

His thumb settled on the pulse racing at the base of her wrist. "Either you are or you have the fastest resting pulse of any human being I've encountered."

She yanked her hand away. "Okay, maybe I am—just a little intimidated. Last night wasn't exactly a great introduction."

"Stand up."

"Pardon me?"

"Stand up."

She eyed him for a moment, then rose to her full five feet eight inches, which, with the added height of her shoes, brought her eyes level with his smooth, perfectly shaven jaw.

"Look at me."

She lifted her gaze, bracing herself for that intimidating stare of his up close, and it was no less formidable than she'd expected it to be. Except she learned there were exotic flecks of amber in it that warmed you up if you dared to look. They disputed the coldness went all the way through him, suggested if he chose to use the full power of that beautiful, complex gaze on you in a particular way for a particular purpose you might melt in his hands like a hundred-plus pounds of useless female.

His mouth tilted. "I'm intense to work with, Francesca, but I'm not the big bad wolf. Nor am I unreasonable. Especially when I've had a full night's sleep."

Right.

"Now say it again like you mean it."

"Say what?"

"I am not afraid of you, Harrison. You're not that scary."

Her mouth twisted. "You're making fun of me."

His sexy mouth curved. "I'm curing you. *Say it.*"

She forced herself to ignore the glitter of humor in his eyes, which took his dangerously attractive vibe to a whole other level. "I am not afraid of you, Harrison. You're not that scary."

"Don't ask me to take that seriously."

She pursed her lips, feeling ridiculous. Injected an iron will into her tone. "I am not afraid of you, Harrison. You're not that scary."

He nodded approvingly. "Better."

His undoubtedly sinfully expensive aftershave worked its way into her pores. They said a person's own chemistry combined with a fragrance to make it what it was and in this case, it was spicy, all male and intoxicating. She wished he would take a step back and relinquish her personal space.

"Francesca?"

"Yes."

His gaze was hooded. Unreadable. "I agree last night was a…disconcerting way to meet. I suggest we wipe it from our memories and start fresh."

The message conveyed was unmistakable. He wasn't just talking about the handcuffs…he was talking about the attraction between them.

She firmed her mouth, taking a step backward. "I think that's an excellent idea. Exactly what I was thinking this morning."

"Good." He waved a hand toward the door. "Back in five. Can we go over the day then?"

She nodded. "Should I really? Call you Harrison, I mean?"

"Tessa does…so yes."

Frankie watched him go, then sat down with the loose limbs of a prisoner who'd just escaped execution and was profoundly grateful for the fact. She found her notebook, carried her tea into Harrison's office and was pondering why Cecily Hargrove hadn't been named Mrs. Harrison Grant yet if he really did have a sense of humor along with the brooding sex appeal, when the phone rang.

She went and picked up the call at her own desk. Leonid Aristov's assistant announced herself briskly and rather snootily. Frankie shifted into Russian, feeling a tug of satisfaction when the other woman paused, took the development in and continued on in her own language. "Mr. Aristov," Tatiana Yankov stated, "would like to have a meeting with Mr. Grant in London next week."

Frankie glanced at Harrison's schedule. "Impossible," she regretted smoothly. If he had time to go to the bathroom it would be a miracle. "Perhaps the last week of August?"

"If Mr. Grant would like to discuss closing this deal with Mr. Aristov, which I believe he is eager to do, he needs to be *in London*, *next week*," the other woman repeated, as if unconvinced of her command of the language.

Frankie kept her tone perfectly modulated. "Could you tell me what this meeting is to be about? That way I can discuss it with Mr. Grant."

"I couldn't say," came the distant response. "Mr. Aristov simply asked me to schedule the meeting. Call me back when you have a date." Tatiana rattled off a London phone number.

Frankie jotted the number down. "I can't schedule a meeting without knowing what it's a—" A dial tone sounded in her ear. She held the phone away from her and stared at it. She had *not* just done that. She was still staring at the phone when Harrison walked past her desk, a steaming cup of coffee in his hand. "Ready?"

She followed him into his office. "That was Leonid Aristov's assistant on the phone."

He wheeled around, coffee sloshing in his mug. Frankie's gaze flew to the boiling liquid as it skimmed the rim of the cup, wavered there like the high seas, then elected to stay in.

"What did she want?"

Frankie returned her gaze to his face. "Aristov wants a meeting next week."

"A meeting?" A frown furrowed his brow. "He's already agreed to everything in principle. Did you ask what the meeting was for?"

"I did. She wouldn't give me anything. She just said Aristov wanted the meeting and it had to be next week."

"Have you had a look at my schedule?" He trained his gaze on her as if she had an IQ of fifty. "This deal is scheduled to pass regulatory authorities next month, Ms. Masseria. I don't fly around the world on a *whim* because Leonid Aristov wants me to."

Great, they were back to *Ms. Masseria*... She closed her eyes and drew a deep breath. "I'm not suggesting you should. But she was very rude. She hung up on me."

He blinked at her. "Why would she hang up on you?"

"She seemed busy. I was trying to probe for more information when she cut me off and hung up."

He impaled her on that razor-sharp gaze of his that had turned him from beauty to the beast in the space of a round second. Then he thrust out an elegant hand. "Give me the number."

She held on to it. "I can call her back. Just give me some direc—"

"Give me the number."

Frankie went back to her desk, grabbed the pink message pad, marched into his office and gave it to him. And called him a bad name in her head. *A big, bad one.* She had liked him so much five minutes ago. She really had.

He was dialing the ice queen back when she left. She put her head down and started working through his email. God forbid she'd missed something they'd need for their briefing.

He came out minutes later. She suppressed a victorious thrill at the dark scowl on his face. "Cancel everything for Thursday and Friday of next week. We'll fly to London Wednesday night, meet with Aristov Thursday morning then leave ourselves a buffer day in case we have more to talk about with him."

"Did you find out what the meeting is for?"

"No," he said icily. "It's all going to be a pleasant surprise."

Frankie kept her eyes on the notepad she was scribbling on. "You said *Wednesday* night we fly out?"

"Yes. Do you have a problem with that?"

'Yes— No—" She lifted her gaze to his in a pained look. "It's just that I have a special—commitment Wednesday night."

His expression darkened. "Taking into account you actually want this job, Ms. Masseria, you will learn to eat, breathe and sleep it for the next six months. So I suggest you…uncommit yourself."

She bit her lip and nodded. If there was one event this year she didn't want to miss, it was Tomasino Giardelli's eightieth birthday party. But this was her job and she needed it. And it had gotten off to a rocky enough start as it was.

"May I ask a question?"

He waved a hand at her.

"I've been working through that last bit of research you wanted Tessa to compile for the Aristov deal. I get what you're asking for, but, well, Coburn always counseled me to understand the big picture so I can visualize what you need in the end product. Give you my best work… What I don't get," she ventured frowning, "is why Grant Industries is buying a company that mirrors the exact capabilities of one of our subsidiaries…"

His jaw went lax. She had the distinct impression he didn't know how to answer her question from the silence that followed. But of course he did, didn't he?

"Coburn," he rasped finally, "and I have different management styles, Ms. Masseria. Coburn likes to collaborate, to involve people in decisions. I don't. I prefer people to *do what I tell them*. That's what works for me."

Not a tyrant? Blood rushed to her face as if he'd physically slapped her. "Fine," she agreed quietly. "If I have a specific question I'll ask it."

"Excellent." He scraped a hand through his hair, looking weary for a man who hadn't yet hit lunch. "Book us a suite at the Chatsfield so we can work."

She nodded. Then, unable to help herself because she needed to get the rules straight, she asked, "Would you prefer me to use Mr. Grant instead of Harrison now that you seem to have reverted to Ms. Masseria?"

He gave her a long, hard look. Frankie's stomach dipped but she held her ground with a lifted chin.

"My slip," he stated in a lethally quiet voice. "First names are fine."

She nodded and turned back to her PC. Harrison started toward his office, then paused outside it. She looked up expectantly.

"We are pursuing Siberius because it commands alternate markets to the ones we already have control of with Taladan. It makes business sense."

"Got it."

He turned to go. She shifted her gaze back to her computer.

"Oh, and, *Francesca*?"

She looked up.

"Please don't write on the bottom half of these." He waved the pink message pad at her. "It distracts me."

He disappeared into his office. Frankie raised her gaze heavenward. Not only did she have to survive life with Harrison Grant for six months, which must prove she was doing penance for something she wasn't yet aware of, she now had to fly across the Atlantic with him for a crucial meeting that seemed shaky in nature.

Nothing could go wrong with that scenario, could it?

At least there weren't air marshals on privately chartered flights...

CHAPTER THREE

FRANKIE ARRIVED AT Teterboro Airport in New Jersey on Wednesday night of the following week as bruised and battered as Rocky Balboa himself after going fifteen rounds with Harrison Grant over the past week. He'd been tense and edgy ever since that call from Leonid Aristov's assistant, pushing them both to the limits of their endurance in ensuring every *i* was dotted and every *t* crossed in advance of their meeting.

She was dead on her feet *and they hadn't even left yet*. Plus, she didn't sleep on planes...

The limousine pulled to a stop on the runway in front of the black-and-red-logoed Grant Industries jet. She slid out and waited while the driver deposited her luggage on the asphalt. If she was curious as to why her boss was obsessed with a deal that, in the great scheme of things, would be a minor acquisition for a behemoth like Grant Industries, she didn't voice her thoughts. She was paid to *do*, apparently. That was all. And if that made her frustratingly aware she wasn't turning in her best work, if she knew she'd do better had he been just a bit more collaborative and explained things fully, there was nothing to be done about it. She had tamed her natural instinct to question.

Survival was the game of the day.

Hand arced over her eyes, she searched for her boss

in the still blinding final rays of the sun. He was standing by the jet speaking to a gray-haired man in his fifties Frankie thought she recognized as the chairman of the senate committee on foreign affairs. She knew this only because her father loved politics and followed it closely, which meant the entire Masseria clan also did so by virtue of association.

The conversation between Harrison and Oliver Burchell looked like more than a friendly hello. *Was he planning a run for the presidency?* The Grant family was as connected as any family in the upper echelons of political power so it absolutely made sense they could put Harrison on every ballot in the country as an independent candidate. But he was only thirty-three. He had his hands full running a company that had just gotten back on its feet. Was now the right timing?

Her boss registered her arrival with that ever-watchful gaze of his. He held up two fingers. Frankie nodded and took the time to study him in a brief, unobserved perusal. She hadn't yet gotten used to how extraordinarily good-looking he was up close. Today, in dark-wash jeans and a crisp white shirt, sleeves rolled up to his elbows to reveal muscular forearms, he looked like her college accounting professor, except where Frankie had considered him nerdily cute, Harrison was a whole other ball game. He was Clark Kent good-looking with his impressive physique and dark designer glasses, as if he was about to dash into a phone booth to go save the world.

Her mouth twisted. Air Force One was about to acquire a whole new sex appeal.

The senator clapped Harrison on the back and moved off toward the plane sitting behind the Grant Industries jet. Frankie pulled in a Harrison-fortifying breath as he strode toward her. "Ready to go?"

"As ready as I'll ever be," she said brightly.

He lifted a brow at her as he stopped in front of her. "I've been that bad?"

She knew when to keep her thoughts to herself. "I meant I'm not a good flyer. I just need to get this over with."

"So I should tell the pilot to lock the doors to the cockpit?"

She made a face at the amusement twisting his lips. "We haven't had one disaster since the coffee incident. Perhaps we can let that joke lie?"

"I'm still keeping my guard up." He pointed their luggage out to the crew who loaded it on to the plane. "You know, statistically speaking," he counseled, gesturing for her to proceed him up the stairs, "flying is safer than any other form of travel. You should be more frightened of getting on the freeway."

"I *am* frightened of getting on the freeway. And fear of flying is not a rational thing," she countered, climbing the steps.

"Ah, but I thought that's what you are…rational Francesca Masseria, who needs to figure out how things work before she fully commits."

She looked down at him from her higher position on the stairs. Who was he really? The big bad wolf or this intuitive, sardonic version of him who made the occasional visit? And did she dare say what she thought?

She exhaled a breath. "I perform better when I have a clear sense of the objectives. I'm more left-brained than Tessa. I need guidance. I can promise if you offer that to me I will give you what you need."

His gaze narrowed. The undercurrent between them that always seemed to simmer below the surface sprang to life. A tutelage of a far different type was filtering through that brilliant mind… She would have bet money on it. Heat rose to her cheeks. He studied the twin spots of fire. Then he turned it off with one of those dismissive looks.

"All right, Francesca Masseria," he drawled. "We'll give it a shot. You've been a good sport this week. I like that about you. You have a question—a *good one*—ask. I'll do my best to answer it."

He strode past her up the stairs and into the jet before she could close her mouth. No way had the beast just thrown her a crumb. She thought maybe they should break out the champagne, particularly when once seated and buckled in opposite Harrison in a bank of four seats, she realized how *small* the plane was. She'd never flown on a private jet before. Coburn preferred to travel on his own and have her work from the office, and this, *this* little plane didn't look hearty enough to carry them across the Atlantic if a storm hit as it had on her last trip to Mexico.

Her shoulders climbed to her ears in protest as the pilot revved the engines.

"Relax," Harrison ordered, pulling his laptop out of his briefcase. "This is going to be the smoothest ride of your life, trust me."

"Now you've jinxed us," Frankie said grimly. She picked up her cell phone to turn it off. He waved a hand at her.

"Not necessary on this flight. You can use the Wi-Fi anytime."

Of course they could. Why waste one usable moment when you could be poring through the stock market? Checking the price of precious metals? She sighed and settled into her seat. Her hope that at some point Harrison's battery might run out had been wishful thinking.

Her phone pinged with a text message. It was from Danny, who was managing Tomasino's party in her absence.

The cake's not here. When is it supposed to arrive?

Frankie frowned and glanced at her watch. An hour ago. Surely her brother hadn't forgotten?

Call the restaurant, she texted back. I'm sure it's on the way.

Harrison looked over at her. "Problems?"

She shook her head. "Just this thing I'm supposed to be at. He'll figure it out."

The attendant came by to check their seat belts and ask what they'd like to drink once they were airborne. Harrison requested a scotch. Frankie gladly followed suit and asked for a glass of wine. Anything that calmed the anxiety clawing its way up her throat was a good thing.

Another text came in. He hasn't left yet. Dammit. Frankie sent a text to her brother Salvatore. Get that cake there, now. You owe me.

"Men," she muttered. Why couldn't they be as buttoned-down as women?

Her boss glanced up from his laptop. "Trust me, he'll be fine. If he has any sense he'll be waiting with an armful of flowers when you get back."

Frankie gave him an uncomprehending look. "Oh—no, it's not that. It's my brother. He's supposed to be delivering a birthday cake to the party I was hosting and he's late."

His dark brows came together. "You were hosting a party?"

"At the church, yes." The engines roared. She kept talking as her pulse skyrocketed. "I host Wednesday night bingo games for the seniors. I've been doing it since I was eighteen. Tomasino Giardelli, whose birthday it is, is like a grandfather to me. It's his eightieth, so we decided to throw him a party and Mama made Tomasino her special tiramisu cake. Which," she added darkly, "he is going to love if Salvatore gets his behind over there with it before it's over. The seniors are wilting as we speak."

"Salvatore?"

"My brother."

A sober look crossed his face. "I'm sorry you're missing the birthday party."

"You didn't know."

"I didn't ask."

She wasn't sure how to respond to that so she looked down at her hands clasped together in a death lock. His gaze sat on her as the jet taxied off to sit in line behind two others. "You really spend every Wednesday night hosting bingo?"

She tightened her seat belt, her heart going pitter-patter as the captain announced they were two minutes to takeoff. "It's always been part of what we do as a family—giving back to the community is important for my parents. It's been good to them."

"Coburn said they have a restaurant in Brooklyn?"

She nodded. 'I'm the youngest of six procreated bus people."

He smiled at that. "Shouldn't you be out on dates instead of hosting bingo? Living the Manhattan single life?"

She made a face. "The last date I was on, the very well-mannered stockbroker I *thought* I was out with accosted me in the elevator on the way down from the restaurant. That was enough for me."

His brows rose. "Accosted?"

Frankie gave an embarrassed wave of her hand. "He kissed me. He wouldn't stop kissing me. And frankly, he was bad at it. I mean, can you imagine?"

The amusement in his eyes deepened. "I can. I mean I *can't* in that he should never have put his hands on you without your permission but the poor guy was probably just desperate."

Frankie crossed her arms over her chest, an image of her flashing him with her lace pull-ups filling her head.

Did he think she usually gave men come-ons like that? She wished she could wipe that entire night from their heads.

"You still don't do that," she said stiffly.

"No," he agreed. "You don't." He gave her a thoughtful look as the jet revved its engines and started down the runway, the speed at which the gray pavement flew by making Frankie light-headed. "Poor-mannered guy aside, there must be a man in your life. You're too attractive for there not to be."

Her chin dipped. "I'm married to my work for the next few years."

"*Or* you're hung up on someone."

The inflection in his voice made her lift her chin and narrow her gaze on him. "No—just not dating."

He shrugged. "Good. Because I'd hate for you to waste your time on my brother, Francesca. He is undoubtedly a magnetic personality and an inspiring leader, but he is not *boyfriend* material by any stretch of the imagination."

Boyfriend material? She blinked at the twin assaults being mounted on her, one from the air as they climbed at a petrifyingly steep angle and one from the man opposite her. "Is that what he thinks? That I have a crush on him?" *Good God.* So she'd responded to a few of her boss's flirtatious smiles lately. She *was* human.

"I can assure you," she said crisply, "I do not have a crush on Coburn."

He held up a hand. "Just a friendly piece of advice. I've seen it happen too many times."

The jet climbed swiftly into the clouds. Frankie gave the receding ground an anxious look, her stomach swooping as the plane rode a current of air. Was that why Coburn had handed her over so easily to Harrison? Because he thought she had a crush on him? That was wrong. So wrong.

A scowl twisted her lips. *Good to know the two Grant brothers both had egos the size of their fortunes...* Her resentment faded to terror as they went through a bumpy patch of cloud, her fingers digging into the armrests.

Harrison sighed and set his computer aside. "You really are terrified of flying."

She clamped down harder on the leather. "Something else to add to my list of eccentricities."

He smiled. "I rather like Rocky. And all joking aside, the seniors, your work in the community, I appreciate your altruism, Francesca. It's refreshing."

"The Grant family does the same."

A cynical light filled his eyes. "There is an intent and purpose behind everything my family does. It's all done with a camera in sight and cleverly crafted messaging at the ready. Hardly the same thing."

His candor caught her off guard. "Hardly surprising with the White House in mind."

He arched a brow at her. "Do we? Have the White House in mind?"

Warmth seeped into her blood-deprived cheeks. "Everyone thinks you do."

He tipped his head at her. "Anyone considering a presidential run spends the years leading up to it coyly denying they're interested. Dropping little hints that never might not mean never, but then again, maybe it does. Then they sit back and take the pulse of every interest group in the nation and see if it's a viable proposition. It's a game, Francesca, a long, bloody battle that would sap the stamina of even the strongest man."

She frowned. So did that mean he was going to or he wasn't?

An elusive smile claimed his lips. "What that means is right now I am focusing on Grant Industries and specifically what Leonid Aristov is going to bring to the table tomorrow."

And with that Harrison Grant cut off whatever valuable insight Frankie might have glimpsed into his psyche and got to work. He pulled up the presentation he'd done for the meeting that addressed two of Aristov's final concerns, asked her to get her notes out and the marathon work session began. This time, however, she was grateful for any distraction that would keep her mind off the fact they were traveling at thirty thousand feet in a glorified tin can.

A couple of hours into their trip across the Atlantic, Harrison thought he might finally have gained some sort of symbiosis with his PA. He could not question Francesca's intelligence after the week they'd just spent together. She was whip-smart, just as Coburn had said, with street smarts to go with it that gave her an uncanny ability to see through people and situations. And now that he'd given her permission to delve deeper with her questions, she was starting to give back to him what he needed—intelligently thought-out ideas on how to present the information she'd gathered to a tricky prospect in Leonid Aristov.

The Russians, he conceded on a deeply exhaled breath, were a thorn in his side. Aristov was playing with him as if he held all the cards when, in fact, he held none. The Russian's fortune was disintegrating in front of his eyes. He *needed* to sell Siberius and yet he was intent on making Harrison's life difficult for a reason he had yet to divulge. Which hopefully, he would wrangle out of him tomorrow.

And Markovic? Well, Markovic was Markovic—an arrogant oligarch with too much money to play with, too flashy a lifestyle and too short a memory to remember the bridges he'd burned. It antagonized Harrison to see him prosper. But soon he would remember what he'd done to his father and he would pay with the same agony Clifford Grant had. With *everything* he had.

Frankie curved one long leg over the other, adjusting her position as he had been over the long flight to keep the blood flowing. It was taking everything *he* had to ignore her five-star legs and keep his mind on work. He might have put a lock on his attraction to her but it didn't mean he wasn't a man with functioning parts. Evidently ones that needed some serious attention.

Coburn would have been highly amused at the situation given his older brother had been born the one with all the self-control and discipline. The one who was not ruled by his emotions. But after a week with Francesca, he almost got why his brother had punted her to him for six months. She was temptation that didn't know it was temptation. And that was the most tempting female of all.

The pilot's voice intruded on his thoughts. *"Hey, folks. We're anticipating some rough weather ahead. I'm going to turn the seat-belt sign on in a few minutes for about an hour so if you'd like to use the restroom, now would be the time."*

A pinched look spread across Frankie's face. "What kind of bad weather?" she asked the attendant as she came to offer them a drink before she sat down.

"A bit of lightning in the area. It could be rough for a while but no worries. Captain Danyon is the best."

Frankie turned a greenish color and unbuckled her seat belt. "Are you okay?" he asked her.

She nodded. "Just going to do like the pilot said."

When she came back, she had a set, determined look on her chalk-white face. They worked through the Aristov presentation. When the captain turned on the seat-belt sign and the bumps began, Frankie kept her gaze fixed on his computer screen and kept talking. As far as storms went, it was a good one. The tiny plane swooped on fast-moving air, then rose again, some of the plunges taking his breath away.

"We can stop," he suggested. "Wait until it's over…"

"Keep talking," she commanded, clutching her seat

with white-knuckled hands. "It's keeping me from freaking out."

He wasn't sure how much she was taking in in her terrified state, but he kept going, working through the back end of the presentation. Forty-five minutes later, they'd finished it and were going through a checklist to make sure they hadn't missed anything crucial.

"We haven't included the most recent market stats," Frankie announced, shuffling through her papers.

"They're on the third slide."

"Oh." She sucked her bottom lip between her teeth and chewed on it. "Do we have that graphic in there, too? The one you asked me to fix and expand?"

"It's in there." He pulled his gaze away from her lush mouth to study her. She didn't look as green as she had earlier, but now she was acting a bit…vague.

"Francesca, are you okay?"

"Perfect." She forced a smile. "I think that's it, then, isn't it? I'll make a note of any questions Aristov asks, although I don't expect he'll have any with this much information put in front of him. Oh—and I'll bring the backup."

The way she said that last part, as if it was a 'nice to have,' alarmed him. "Yes," he said deliberately, "the backup is key. We can't forget the backup."

"No problem." She rubbed her palm across her forehead. "Can we talk about the shareholder meetings now? I really need to get a handle on them."

"If you're a hundred percent clear on the meeting, yes."

"A hunnndred percent, yes." She nodded and tucked the folder in her briefcase and pulled out her notepad. "So for the shareholder thing…"

"Meetings," he corrected. Had she just *slurred* that word? Or was she being funny?

"Right. The meetings… They cover the Monday and

Tuesday, right? With the Wednesday afternoon kept for additional items that come up?"

"The *Tuesday* afternoons are for open items, yes. The meetings are over Tuesday night."

She blinked at him. "That's what I said. Tuesday."

"You said Wednesday. It's *Tuesday* for the open session. Here." He pulled the schedule from her unopened folder. "Look at this."

She studied it with the glazed-eyed look of someone who wasn't taking anything in. "Got it." A sigh escaped her. She put her elbows on the table and rubbed her eyes. "I'm so sorry. My head is very cloudy all of a sudden."

A wave of guilt spread through him. "You're probably exhausted. It's been a long week."

"Yes, but this..." She put her palms to her temples. "I think I might need to lie down."

He pulled her hands away from her face. "You're not feeling well?"

"I'm fine...it's just—" Her bleary gaze skipped away from his. "I—I took a pill my sister gave me for the turbulence. It's making me..."

"Where is it?"

"In my purse."

He grabbed her bag off the seat, opened it up and plucked the pill bottle off the top. Scanning the label he saw it was a sedative.

"Have you taken these before?"

"No. I didn't think they'd hit me this hard." She plopped her chin in her palms, elbows braced on the table, and closed her eyes. "Maybe it'll wear off in a few minutes. Maybe I should have some coffee."

"How many did you take?"

"Just one. But I feel...light-headed."

He uttered a low curse. "It's going to last for hours. You need to lie down."

"I'd rather have some coffee."

He stripped off his seat belt, rounded the table and undid hers. Her eyes half opened. "The seat-belt sign is—"

"Shut up." He slipped his arms underneath her knees and back and lifted her up. She was surprisingly light for a female with her curves, and it should have been an easy carry to the bedroom at the back of the jet, but the plane was dipping and swaying beneath his feet and it was all he could do to keep his balance. Her fingers dug into his biceps with a strength born of fear, her body trembling in his arms.

He kept her braced against his chest as he negotiated the door handle to the bedroom, shouldered himself in and deposited her on the bed with a lucky move that brought him down hard beside her. The jet dropped, this time a good fifty feet, pulling a low, agonized cry from Francesca. He kept a hand on her, his body half draped over her. The jet leveled out. "Swallow," he commanded.

Her throat convulsed as she did. "This is soooo not good."

"It's just turbulence." He recovered his own breath.

"Still." Her eyes popped open, valiantly hanging on to her terror. "Donnn't leave me."

"I can't at this moment." He gave the sky a grim look through the tiny, oval windows. It was an inky, endless black canvas crisscrossed by vibrant streaks of jagged gold lightning.

Francesca pulled him toward her as if he was a pillow. He put a palm to her shoulder to push her back into the bed. A whimper escaped her throat. "Please."

He crumbled. Gathered her soft curves to him and held her while the storm raged on outside. She smelled like orange blossoms—like intoxication and innocence all in one. The plane leveled out and stayed that way for minutes. In the warmth of his arms, Francesca stopped trembling. He tried to remember the last time he'd held a woman like this, for comfort, and didn't have to think long. It would have been seven years ago when Susanna had left.

The thought did something strange to his head. He glanced out the window as the lightning receded and the space between rumbles of thunder lengthened. Having Francesca wrapped around him like this was inspiring the need to find out whether his dream would come anything close to reality... The thought made him hard so fast, comfort was obliterated on a long, potent surge of lust.

He stood and dumped her on the bed. Her eyes flickered open. "It's calming down now." She curled up in the fetal position and used the pillow as a cushion instead of him. He turned and made for the door as a whole lot more creamy thigh was exposed. *Mother of God.*

Back in the main cabin, he buckled himself in and stared out the window at the storm. He'd called this one—he had. It had been a bad idea. A bad idea that was getting worse every minute.

CHAPTER FOUR

FRANKIE WOKE WITH the instinctive feeling something was not quite right. Bright light beat an assault against the throb behind her eyes. Her head felt fuzzy...*heavy*.

She closed her eyes harder against the overwhelming light. She must have forgotten to close the blinds. And on a morning when she had a blinding headache... *Great*.

A low, insistent hum beneath her ear made her frown. Were they renovating the brownstone across the street *again*? The floor dipped beneath her, riding a stream of air. *Floors don't move unless you live in California*. Her eyes sprang open. The light streaming in was coming from tiny oval windows, a world of blue flowing by. She wasn't in her bedroom; she was in the Grant Industries jet on her way to London. And it was morning.

Her gaze flew to the watch on her arm—*8:00 a.m. Oh, lord*.

Pieces of the night before assembled themselves in her head. That awful thunder and lightning storm... The way the jet had been tossed around like a toy airplane, subjected to God's fury. That pill of her sister's she'd taken that had knocked the lights out of her...

Oh, no. Her heart plummeted. The rest of it she didn't *want* to remember. Her boss carrying her in here in the middle of that madness because she'd been half passed out. Him putting her to bed. Him holding her...

She buried her face in the pillow. She'd clung to him like a woman possessed. So far from the independent, strong woman she was it made her cringe to think of it. Made her cringe to think she'd given him yet another reason to think her less than competent.

Heat flooded her face. Tessa would never have put herself in that position. Tessa would have been cool as a cucumber in the face of almost certain aeronautic death.

She got out of bed in a hurry, made it behind her and attempted to straighten her rumpled suit and hair. Deciding nothing was actually going to be accomplished until she changed clothes and redid her makeup, she made her way out into the main cabin.

Harrison looked fresh in a crisp blue linen shirt, tie and pants, his jacket slung over the back of the seat beside him. *Ready to do battle with Leonid Aristov.*

He looked up at her. "Feeling better?"

She nodded. "I apologize for last night. I had no idea that pill was going to affect me that way."

He waved a hand at her. "Forget about it. It was a bad storm." He flicked a glance at his watch. "We're landing in just over an hour. If you want to shower and change, do it now."

She nodded. She wanted desperately to tell him this wasn't *her*, not the way she'd been acting lately. But he stuck his head back in the report he was reading. Not the time to plead her case. And a part of her knew with Harrison, actions spoke louder than words.

She retraced her steps to the bedroom and headed for the shower to make herself into the deadly efficient assistant she knew she was. She could do this. She could.

They landed without incident at London City Airport, where they were picked up by a car and spirited to the Chatsfield. The opulence of the swanky hotel with its reputation for hosting anyone who mattered bounced off Harrison's consciousness as they were ushered up to their luxury suite. His mind was focused on the meeting ahead and getting Leonid Aristov to sign on the dotted line.

He checked his smartphone as Francesca dropped her belongings in her bedroom. An email had come in from Aristov. A feeling of foreboding swept over him.

Grant—Stuck in Brussels. I'm hosting a charity gala tonight at my house in Highgate. Why don't you come and we'll talk there? Two tickets will be delivered to you this afternoon. L

Rage bubbled up inside of him, swift and all-consuming. Was he kidding? He had dragged himself across an ocean, put together an exhaustive presentation that obliterated the Russian's concerns about the acquisition and he wanted to talk at a *party*?

His brain whirred as he struggled to figure out why Aristov was suddenly putting this deal on the back burner when he had been so anxious to sign just weeks ago. Forty million dollars was going to go a long way to pulling the Russian out of the financial mess the oligarch had found himself in recently, bad luck and bad decisions plaguing him in his home country and threatening the empire he'd built.

He shoved his hands in his pockets and walked to the floor-to-ceiling windows with their incomparable view of London, agitation raising his pulse rate. Aristov had told him he was getting out of the automotive business and realigning his assets. *So why?*

A niggling worry entered his head, one he hadn't let himself think of until now. Could Aristov have guessed his true intentions? That acquiring Siberius was only a stepping stone to destroying the man who had killed his father? *Impossible*. He had made sure every company, every lifeline he had snapped up that kept Anton Markovic's automotive empire in business had been buried so deep behind red tape they could never be traced back to him. The one or two deals he'd made publicly could innocently be explained as smart business strategy.

That Siberius was the only supplier in the world left that could keep Anton Markovic manufacturing engines once Grant Industries cut off his other lifelines was something Aristov could not know.

His head pounded with a deep throb, drawing his hand to his skull. If he didn't obtain Siberius as planned, Markovic would continue production, the Russian's company would gain more influence and his plan would be dead in the water.

A fiery feeling stirred to life low in his gut. He would never let that happen, not while he lived and breathed on this earth.

His head took him back to that night. To the horrific scene that had met him when he had walked into the Grant family home on the eve of his father's announcement he would run for governor. The unnatural silence in the house. The eerie feeling that something was very, very wrong. His father's body had been limp and lifeless, slumped over the desk he had created such genius at.

His body went rigid. The beast in him climbed out of the box he had placed it in seven years ago and into his head, blurring his vision. Anton Markovic had been as responsible for his father's death as if he had pulled the trigger himself and he would have a target on his back until he lived his own personal version of hell.

There was no other possible outcome.

The gray mist in his head swirled darker. He pushed it ruthlessly away. If he let the wolves in his head win, if he let the beast rule, he would make a mistake. And any wrong move at this point would bring it all crashing down.

Francesca chose that particular moment to walk back into the room. Her apprehensive expression as he turned to face her had him wiping the emotion clean from his face.

"Is something wrong?"

"Aristov is stuck in Brussels. He wants to discuss the deal at a gala party he's throwing in Highgate tonight."

Her eyes widened. She wisely held her counsel. He turned back to the windows to study the city he'd flown thousands of miles to reach only to be slapped in the face by Leonid Aristov. He could fly back to the States tonight and be done with it, or he could make one more attempt to try and figure out what was going on in Aristov's complicated head.

The thought that regulators would be looking at the deal *in weeks* had him turning around.

"Go buy yourself a dress. We have a party to attend."

CHAPTER FIVE

THE MOST EXPENSIVE dress she had ever bought, *times ten*, floating around her ankles, hair tamed into a sophisticated up-do by the Chatsfield salon staff and some simple makeup in place, Frankie finally allowed herself a look in the mirror. Her eyes nearly bugged out of her head.

The haute-couture-clad, *daring* stranger that stared back at her was not the Frankie Masseria she knew. She would never in a million years have bought this dress if the saleswoman had not insisted it was exactly right for "Leonid Aristov's party of the year."

"Anyone who is anyone is going to be there, sweetheart. Trust me, you cannot be ordinary."

So here she was, anything but ordinary, and not at all sure she could carry it off. Ordinary had been her mantra her entire life. Sure, she had a killer figure; reactions from men had told her that. But she didn't have her two sisters' striking blue eyes to go with her dark hair. She was not a doctor, psychologist, chemical engineer or entrepreneur. She was the girl her mother sent in to calm a particularly difficult customer when no one else could. She and her nondescript GPA had been so good at it her parents had urged her to stay in the family business. But she hadn't wanted to do it. She'd wanted to become a somebody. And coming to work at Grant Enterprises had made her *feel* like a somebody.

She gave her appearance another assessing look. The dress, a stunning, smoky blue color the salesperson had said perfectly matched her eyes clung to every inch of her body as though it had been painted on. But because of the way the beautiful material slipped elusively away from her skin, it was come-hither rather than tacky.

What had sealed the deal, though, and made her set Harrison's black-label credit card down on the counter was the back of the dress. The gorgeous cutout that revealed the graceful sweep of her shoulder blades and much of her back was sexy yet ladylike.

A knock sounded on the connecting door. Her nerves amped up another notch or two. *Harrison.* Tessa had been right. You could have timed the Swiss train system after him, he was that punctual.

Wary of keeping the beast waiting, she picked up her wrap, draped it around her shoulders and swung the door open. Her breath stopped somewhere in her chest. He looked obscenely handsome in a tux that was undoubtedly as expensively made as her dress, the elegant formal wear a perfect foil for his clean-edged, dark masculinity.

She looked up at him before her gaping became obvious. But he was too busy looking at her to notice. His dark gaze seemed to be caught in a state of suspended animation as it moved over her, taking in the daring dress. And he didn't remove it right away. The full-on stare went on for a good three or four seconds, sending a wave of heat through her. Unlike some men's open admiration that had, in the past, made her feel uncomfortable, Harrison's stare made her feel *unbalanced.*

He cleared his throat. "You look…beautiful."

His uncharacteristic struggle for words unleashed a fluttery feeling deep in her stomach. *Stop it,* she told herself. *He's your boss. Now is the time to act cool and collected so he knows you can actually do it.*

"I hope it's not too much," she offered casually. "The saleslady said it was perfect for tonight."

"It's not too much." He looked as if he was going to say something else, then clamped his mouth shut. "We should go."

The ride to Highgate was smooth and quiet as London flashed by the tinted windows of the Rolls-Royce. Harrison was silent, a frown etched in his brow, formulating a plan of attack for Leonid Aristov, no doubt. Her nerves skyrocketed as they entered the exclusive London suburb. Georgian homes shook hands with fascinating Victorian Gothic structures. Not to be outdone, a handful of architecturally brilliant modern homes made their own statement on the tree-lined street.

All impressive, but it was Leonid Aristov's Georgian Revival mansion that was the most impressive of all. Tucked between a canopy of trees as they climbed the hill, the redbrick mansion stood white-pillared and regal on rolling acres. Massive. She'd read it contained fifty-two rooms, including eighteen bedrooms and ten bathrooms, an Imperial-inspired ballroom and an underground bath that harked back to Roman times. As they continued to climb, she stared up at the structure gleaming with light. She'd never seen anything like it.

When they reached the top of the hill, they turned a corner and accessed the property from the official entrance off a quiet road cradled in the branches of giant oak trees. Limousines pulled to a halt in a parade of arrivals in the circular driveway.

Frankie tugged the low bodice of her dress up and checked her hair for the tenth time as they waited in the queue. Harrison shot her a quelling glance. "Stop fidgeting. You look perfect."

She stuck her hands back in her lap. "I suppose you do this once a week."

A fleeting smile crossed his lips. "Not once a week. Remember—they are people like you."

Her heart did a little flip. He was breathtaking when he smiled. How had she ever thought Coburn the better-looking brother? Where Coburn was stunning in a flashy, attention-getting way, Harrison was devastating in a complex, unforgettable way. He had about fifty layers. She wondered if anyone ever got to the bottom of them. It made a woman want to try, that was for sure.

She removed her gaze from him. The only lover she'd had was a year-long relationship two years ago in college. What did she know about unpeeling layers? *Heavens.* She needed to focus on keeping her job, not unraveling her boss in a very distracting way.

The car slid forward to the pillared entrance. A white-gloved, uniformed staff member stepped forward to open the door. "Welcome to Gvidon House."

Harrison stepped out and offered her his hand. She took it and emerged into the flashing bulbs of paparazzi cameras. He leaned down to her. "Gvidon House?"

She blinked against the blinding lights and rested her hand on his arm for balance. "He's a prince from a Russian fairy tale. Apparently Leonid is a big fan of them."

"Fairy tales?"

She nodded, settling her weight firmly on two feet as she eyed the red carpet. It seemed long and never ending.

Harrison set a hand to the small of her back to guide her toward it. "How do you know that?"

"I did my research."

He gave her a measuring look. "Then you know his current girlfriend is Juliana Rossellini, who works for one of London's top auction houses."

"Who is fifteen years his junior."

He nodded. "See if you can gain some intelligence about Leonid from her."

She would, but right now she was too consumed by the distracting feeling of his palm on the bare skin of her back as the handlers indicated they could start down the carpet. It was big and warm. Comforting yet disconcerting at the same time.

His fingers increased their pressure on her skin. "Relax. Pretend it's a walk in the park. You're smelling the flowers…enjoying yourself."

The park didn't have fifty cameras stuck in her face. The park hadn't just realized it was Harrison on the carpet, causing an unexpected buzz. They called his name as they moved forward. Frankie stuck the fakest smile of her life on her lips and held it.

"What if they connect us in the photo?"

His mouth quirked. "It wouldn't do my reputation any harm having a stunning brunette on my arm. I've apparently been going through a dry spell."

A stunning brunette. A flush she was certain would show up in the photographs deepened her cheeks. She was quite sure she didn't compare to any of his beautiful escorts. She'd seen them. They were way out of her league.

"Does it bother you?" she asked. "Being in a constant media spotlight?"

He shrugged. "It's been my life. You get used to it."

They made it down the carpet without incident to the entrance where a queue was forming. People were removing their wraps, shoes… "Metal detector," one of the greeters explained.

A metal detector?

Frankie looked around for something to hold on to while she took off her shoes. Harrison held out his elbow. "Why is it always the women's shoes?" she complained.

His mouth curled. "Because they are weapons. With you, they could be a dangerous thing."

She made a face at him. They made it through the metal

detector unscathed and were directed to the terrace where the cocktails were being served. Frankie was gobsmacked by the scene. Some guests were milling about the exquisitely landscaped, multilevel terrace in the same formal wear she and Harrison had on, jewels dripping from their necks and ears. Others were lounging in the pool in bathing suits, cocktails in hand.

Her eyes widened at the sight of a diamond-encrusted blonde in the pool across the bridge. She was pretty sure those were real diamonds making up the hardly there bikini. They were just too sparkly not to be.

"Apparently," she murmured to Harrison, "I just needed to bring my bathing suit. It would have been a lot cheaper."

He gave her one of his dark, fathomless looks. "I think you're a lot safer in the dress."

The heat that passed between them was swift and unmistakable. She bit the inside of her mouth. *Unfair*, her eyes told him. *I thought we were playing by the rules.*

You asked for that one, his gaze flashed in return. *Be honest.*

She wanted to say she had no experience playing this game. That she was merely attempting to keep her job by attending this party. But he was already scouting the crowd. "Let's make our way to the bar. We can look for our hosts along the way."

They weren't more than a few feet into the crowd when Harrison spotted Aristov. He nodded his head toward the far pool. "He's in a tux, Juliana's in a red dress." Frankie found the couple easily, having also looked at photos of Leonid Aristov during her research. They stood out even among this decadent crowd with their superior, distinctive good looks. A definite power couple.

Harrison acquired a drink for them at the bar, then they wound their way around the candle-strewn lively pools until they were close enough to greet Aristov when he was finished his conversation. It was a good twenty minutes before the Russian made his way over to them with his entourage. She could feel Harrison's powerful body gaining heat beside her with every minute that passed.

Harrison and Leonid exchanged greetings. Leonid, a tall, thin Russian with whiskey-colored eyes and a craggy attractive face, gave Frankie a kiss on each cheek, then introduced his tall, statuesque girlfriend, Juliana, and his second in command, Viktor Kaminski. Juliana was a jaw-droppingly beautiful brunette with just enough imperfections to make her fascinating. She gave Harrison an appreciative look as he kissed her on each cheek, then greeted Frankie. Viktor Kaminski, a ruddy-cheeked, slightly paunchy, not attractive Russian, brought Frankie's hand to his mouth. "How lucky for Harrison," he murmured against her fingers.

She retrieved her hand but couldn't escape Viktor's ardent admiration, particularly when Harrison mentioned she spoke Russian. He insisted she try it out with him while he told her all about the magnificent paintings up for auction that evening, a subject she knew nothing about but feigned interest in.

Thankfully she and Juliana, who was unpretentious and lovely, hit it off. When Leonid offered to introduce Harrison around, Juliana grabbed her hand. "I'll take Francesca to get another glass of champagne. You are so *boring* when you talk business."

"Good thing I shine in other areas," Leonid came back with one of his crooked smiles.

Juliana gave him a saucy look as she took Frankie's arm and led her through the crowd. "Two powerful, delicious men," she murmured. "They look good together."

She couldn't argue with that.

At the bar, Juliana claimed two seats. Frankie sat down beside her. "Poor Viktor," Juliana teased, "he so has the hots for you. But who would be interested in him when your boss looks like Harrison?"

"I'd like to keep my job."

Juliana's dark eyes sparkled. "You can always find another job…"

Not like hers. Not when she'd worked so hard to prove she could be a success. She hadn't performed a ground-breaking open-heart surgery like her brother Emilio had.

Juliana caught the bartender's attention and ordered them champagne. "Leonid says Harrison has big political ambitions…that a presidential run isn't out of the question."

"I wouldn't mention that to him," Frankie said drily. "He'll feed you a whole spiel about how presidential candidates don't really *run*. They *lurk*."

"Still." Juliana gave her a meaningful look. "Power is an aphrodisiac. And *he* is delicious."

"He's not hard to look at."

"There's tension between him and Leonid," Juliana observed.

She kept her smile even. "I think Harrison is just anxious to close the deal. There seems to be a couple of minor sticking points."

Juliana snorted. "I think they're too much *alike*, that's the problem. Leonid likes to be in control. So does Harrison. They're alpha dogs of the highest order. Even if Leonid's empire is crumbling in a very public way, his ego needs to be stroked."

Frankie wasn't sure that was in the cards.

The bartender laid two glasses of champagne on the bar. Juliana slid one over to Frankie. "People might find it hard to believe, but it's not all about business with Leonid. Tonight is about him doing good. He is a *good* man. He needs to feel the decisions he's making are right. So if something is holding him back with Harrison's deal at this late stage, it's not about what's on paper, it's about what's in his heart."

Frankie filed that away for future use. "What's he like?" she asked Juliana curiously. "Leonid? He seems like such an enigma."

The brunette's lips curved. "Very much so. Mensa-level IQ. Hard. Tough as nails. But good to his friends, good to those who work for him and a marshmallow with me despite the fact his ex-wife took half his money and ran."

"One of the good oligarchs, then."

Juliana nodded. "Unlike some. Anton Markovic, for instance." She gave a delicate shiver. "I wouldn't have him in this house if Leonid didn't do business with him."

Frankie knew of Markovic, of course. He was one of the world's richest men, two places higher on the list than Harrison last year. "Is he here?"

"He's out of the country, thank goodness. I don't have to pretend I like him."

"Why *don't* you like him?"

The smile faded from the brunette's face. "He's dangerous. Far too many underworld connections, far too nasty and far too unfriendly to his women."

Frankie made a mental note to avoid Anton Markovic if she ever came into contact with him. Which was unlikely since this was probably the last time she'd ever be at a party like this.

"Anyway," Juliana said, holding her glass up to Frankie's, "enough about business. *Cin-cin*."

Frankie sipped her champagne slowly as Juliana introduced her around. But the spirit hit her quickly as it always did. By the time Juliana delivered her to Harrison the better part of an hour later, she was in a much more relaxed mood. Harrison, unfortunately, was not. Leonid was not with him and it was clear from the tense set of her boss's jaw he had yet to have the talk he needed to have with the Russian.

Juliana left them to facilitate the auction that was to begin shortly and Viktor disappeared to greet a guest. Harrison threw back the last swallow of whatever amber liquid he was drinking and scowled. "I have no idea why we came. He's been avoiding me, pawning me off on his guests when he knows I want to talk to him."

Frankie thought about what Juliana had said. Did she dare speak up or would that be the last straw for her and Harrison? She pressed her empty glass to her chin and surveyed the beast at his most riled. She had valuable information. She needed to tell him.

She took a deep breath. "Juliana said with Leonid it's not all about business. That he needs to feel good about the decisions he's making. She said if something is holding him back with this deal, it's not about what's on paper, it's about what's in his heart."

The deadly stare he directed at her made Frankie shift her weight to both feet. *"You discussed the deal with her?"*

Her chin snapped up. *"You* asked me to feel her out. She was the one to bring it up. She could sense the tension between you two."

He muttered an oath under his breath. She stood her ground, palms moist, knees shaky as he turned and prowled over to stare into one of the cascading pools. "He doesn't need to feel good about the bloody deal," he growled. "It's going to save his hide."

"And what's going to save his pride?" Frankie returned softly. "Leonid is in financial difficulty. His empire is suffering a very public defeat, yet he throws a party like this one tonight to make a gesture. It sends a message that he is not bowed by it. That he will survive. Let him see you understand that. *Show him* you understand."

He turned around, a savage light in his gaze. "This is all from Juliana?"

She quaked a little inside. "Yes."

He scowled. "Even if I could show him I *understand*, how can I do it when he won't talk? He is never alone. Kaminski hasn't left his goddamned side for a minute."

"There has to be an opportunity." Frankie had always been a glass-half-full kind of person. "Juliana said the auction is very important to Leonid. He wants it to go well. Maybe he's keyed up about it and you'll have your chance afterward."

"Or maybe it's another *giant waste of my time*."

"You won't know until you try."

The glass-half-full part of her hoped she was right.

He stared hard at her. Deposited his empty glass on the table. "Let's go, then."

The over-the-top ballroom done in gold and imperial red was buzzing with anticipation when they arrived. Again, as it seemed with all of Leonid Aristov's estate, it was like nothing she'd ever seen before. Slavic in feel, it dripped with ornate, antique chandeliers, featuring a half-dozen tiny balconies that opened to a view over the man-made lake Leonid had created. All of the little balconies reminded Frankie of the inside of a Russian opera house.

Tuxedo-clad waiters circulated with trays of champagne to whet the appetites of bidders, while staff passed out gold embossed lists of the items up for auction.

The list would have been impressive, she was sure, if Frankie had known anything more about art than Viktor Kaminski had bent her ear with earlier. Her eyes nearly bugged out of her head when she saw the opening bids for some of the paintings. They were in the millions.

"Wow," she murmured. "This is the real deal."

Harrison didn't respond. He was scanning the list with a furrowed brow.

The lights went up. Leonid took the stage and welcomed everyone, Juliana at his side. He made a joke about her not being up for auction with his dry humor that drew an amused response from the crowd. Frankie found his speech about his commitment to the arts and the artists who continued to make the world a more beautiful place heartfelt and eloquent. She could see the goodness in him Juliana had talked about. It made the charismatic Russian even more attractive and compelling.

Leonid highlighted a few of the marquee items up for auction, then exited the stage to be replaced by Juliana's auctioneer. The Brit with his booming voice began the auction with some paintings by a new modern Russian artist. The value of the works continued to go up with every item, with the last painting selling for two million pounds.

A Chagall in brilliant blue tones came next. "I love that one," she murmured to Harrison. It was, according to the brochure, "a piece from one of the artist's most famous series set in Nice, featuring his famous sirens."

Harrison nodded. "I like it, too."

The bidding for the painting started at one and a half million pounds. A Brit in the front row signaled two. A determined look on his face, an American with a Southern accent took it up to two and a half million. The two men went back and forth until the price tag sat at three and a half million.

Harrison raised his hand. "Four million."

Frankie gaped at him. *"Four million,"* the auctioneer crowed, "by the gentleman in the back."

The auctioneer tried to persuade the other bidders to up the price, but the American and Brit weren't biting. *Apparently they were sane.*

"Sold," sang the auctioneer, "for four million pounds to Mr. Grant in the back."

The ballroom was a buzz of conversation. Frankie looked at Harrison, her astonishment written across her face.

"It was a gesture," he said roughly. "And I like the painting."

A four-million-pound gesture. Two more paintings were sold, an astonishing amount of money changed hands, then Leonid appeared back on stage to thank the guests for their generosity and wrap the proceedings. When he stepped down from the stage, said something to Viktor Kaminski and slipped into the crowd, Harrison's gaze tracked him. The Russian was finally alone.

He turned to her. "Can you occupy Kaminski for a few minutes?"

She knew what he was asking, knew it was well past her job description, but tonight she wanted to show Harrison Grant what she was made of. "No problem," she replied crisply, smoothing her dress over her hips. "Leave him to me."

He nodded and strode off after Leonid. Frankie kept her eyes on Viktor as he spoke to the auctioneer. When he left him and headed to the opulent bar, done in exotic dark woods and stone, she headed through the crowd and discreetly shouldered her way to the front of the line. She emerged to the right of Viktor, who had his forearms on the bar and was chatting with one of the attractive servers. She trained her gaze on the bartender as he took her order, hoping Viktor would notice her. But the Russian was lazily engaged with the attractive blonde, chatting for a few moments with her before she heard him order two cognacs. *One for Leonid.*

Adrenaline surged through her. She raised her voice beyond her usual soft, modulated tone as she thanked the bartender for the soda and lime. Viktor glanced over at her, his eyes lighting up as if he'd struck gold in the Yukon.

He wrapped his fingers around the two glasses of cognac that sat on the bar and made his way over to her. "You shouldn't be getting your own drink," he chastised. "Where's Grant?"

"Talking to an acquaintance." She adopted as arch a look as her limited repertoire allowed. "Maybe I can take you up on your offer to show me Leonid's art collection while he's occupied? I'm so inspired after the auction. It's all so beautiful…"

Viktor flicked a glance toward the balconies. His frown belied his indecision. "Pretty please," she murmured, laying it on thick. "I'll never get another chance like this."

He gave her an indulgent look. "Only if you agree to experience what a nineteenth-century Frapin Cuvée tastes like." He held up the cognac. "I was on my way to meet Leonid."

"Done," she murmured. She had one more glass of tolerance in her.

She picked up the glass, took the arm Viktor offered and they made their way through the crowd to the long marble hallway that stretched the second floor of the manor. Aristov's art collection, Viktor explained, was displayed along this and the grand hallway of the third floor. Frankie could see why. The Oriental-carpeted, ornately wainscoted hallways and expert lighting set the artwork off to perfection.

She didn't have to feign attention. Viktor took her through each piece with an enthusiasm that was infectious. His clear love for his subject matter shone through and understanding what she was looking at made it so much more enjoyable for her. She put her hand on his arm frequently to indicate her pleasure, smiling up at him with exaggerated fascination. She could see it was working, from his animated expression and heightened color in his cheeks.

A surge of feminine power heated her veins. She really wasn't half-bad at this femme fatale thing. Why hadn't she tried it before?

Viktor took her through the artwork on the second, then third floors. By the time he stopped in front of what he called the *pièce de résistance*, an exceedingly modern piece by one of the great Russian masters that looked like random splotches of black and green to Frankie, a good twenty minutes had gone by.

"It's so…interesting," she commented, cradling her cognac in her hands. She was sipping the five-thousand-dollar-a-bottle spirit as slowly as she could, but its faint spiciness and floral aroma was delicious, sending a smooth, silky warmth through her bloodstream.

"It's breathtaking," Viktor countered, resting a palm against the wall where she stood. "I really should get back. Leonid is waiting for me."

"Oh," she murmured in disappointment, not sure they'd been gone long enough. "I was hoping there was more."

The Russian's eyes flashed. "There is an even more glorious Chagall in Leonid's personal rooms. I'm sure he won't mind me showing it to you."

Alarm bells went off in Frankie's head. The expression of intent in Viktor's light brown eyes was clear. He was so close she could smell his overwhelming aftershave, a spicy combination that made her want to sneeze.

"Oh, no," she said quickly. "I wouldn't dare intrude on Leonid's personal space."

"Are you sure?" He moved closer. "You've been such a good audience."

"Yes," she said firmly. She put a hand to the wall to lever herself away from it, but Viktor stepped closer, stopping her. *He was going to kiss her.* She'd been flirting outrageously with him to keep his attention, so why wouldn't he?

Her heart raced. "Viktor...this has been so sweet of you to give me a tour but—"

He set his other hand on the wall beside her so she was well and truly captured. "Don't run away," he said in Russian, his voice low and gravelly. "Stay."

Panic sliced through her. He dipped his head toward hers. She ducked under his arm and took a step away from him. He gave her a bemused look. Frankie held up her almost empty glass. "I think I need another one of these first."

He eyed her glass. "Another?"

She nodded enthusiastically. "It was sooo delicious. Just one more."

His generous mouth curved into a smile. "We'll make a full Russian out of you yet with that...*appetite*."

Her stomach did a little churn. Then relaxed as he good-naturedly held out an arm and led the way back down the hallway to the stairs and the ballroom below. He kept a possessive hand on her back as they wound their way through the crowd toward the bar. Frankie searched furiously for Harrison while he got their drinks, but the crowds were thick now, massed on the dance floor with a strobe light passing over them. She couldn't see him anywhere.

Viktor came back with their drinks, handing one to her. "We should dance," he announced.

Frankie thought that might be a good idea because she really didn't need any more to drink. She went to put the glass down on a table. Viktor waved a hand at her. "Bring it with you."

He led her onto the dance floor, where the band was playing a slow enough tune that they could dance and drink at the same time. She fake-sipped the cognac as Viktor's free hand around her waist kept her close. The champagne she'd consumed combined with the first cognac had cast the world in an all-over rosy glow, which would have been nice except *this* was a bit of a nightmare. The dance floor was packed, the heat of hundreds of bodies was magnifying her partner's überstrong cologne and he kept moving her closer with his free hand. She had the feeling he was going to try and kiss her again any minute...

Goddamn you, Harrison Grant. Where are you?

CHAPTER SIX

LEONID ARISTOV WAS a solitary figure on the balcony that overlooked the lake. His elbows rested on the marble ledge that bounded the tiny alcove; his tall, thin body tilted forward as he studied the play of light on the water in the moonlight.

He did not seem at all surprised when Harrison joined him at the railing. His trademark crooked smile flashed white in the darkness. "A Chagall fan? I had no idea."

"Always have been." Harrison rested his forearms on the ledge, mimicking the other man's stance.

"And here I thought you were above trying to impress me."

He lifted a shoulder. "Call it a gesture of good faith. I'm trying to understand the backpedaling, Leonid. I thought we had an agreement."

A laconic smile curved the Russian's lips. "I'm like a bride on my wedding day. I'm having second thoughts."

"About the two insignificant clauses you keep tripping over?"

"I don't care about those."

"Then what?" Harrison kept his temper in check, recalling Francesca's words. "Help me to understand."

Leonid stared out at the water. "A man gets philosophical when his life's work is crumbling at his feet. What was once important to me has become less so."

Harrison's gaze sharpened on the Russian's craggy profile. "You've made a few questionable decisions, Leonid. You're a brilliant businessman. You will rise from the ashes."

"As you did." Aristov flicked him a sideways glance. "My gut tells me this deal is not about Siberius, Harrison. It's about Anton Markovic and your desire to make him pay. The crowning act of your ascension back to glory."

Alarm rocketed through him. *How could the Russian know?* It was impossible. *Impossible.* But somehow, his mind raggedly conceded, he did.

He kept his face expressionless. "Why would you think this has anything to do with Markovic? That's ancient history."

Aristov turned to him, pinning him with the full force of that whiskey-hard gaze. "Because Markovic has become one of the most powerful men in the world. He put your father in his grave...*I* would want him to suffer." His lips twisted at the confusion in Harrison's eyes. "A few questions to a friend in Mergers and Acquisitions at a major investment bank and I had my answers. I know you've purchased another key supplier of Markovic's. I put two and two together."

A red mist descended over his vision, fury mixing with a fear that froze him solid. Heads would roll if it was discovered a banker had divulged that type of information. But that didn't matter now... He had a way bigger problem. Leonid and Anton Markovic did business together. If Leonid chose to, he could blow his entire plan out of the water.

Why hadn't he done so already?

"I can't stand Markovic." Leonid answered his unspoken question. "Yes, I do business with him but you can't always pick your dance partners. My issue," he drawled, "is not what you choose to do to Markovic. I would take

pleasure in watching him fall. It's Siberius and your ultimate plans for it I care about."

Relief poured through him, slackening his limbs. He
lifted his shoulder in a casual shrug. "It becomes a complementary subsidiary to Taladan that gives Grant International access to the markets we need."

"Or it becomes extraneous. Superfluous...*nonexistent.*"
Aristov's gaze narrowed. "The market coverage Siberius
brings to the table is not robust beyond the Slavic countries. You may choose to simply fold it into your megalith
and it becomes a distant memory."

He kept his expression neutral as Aristov read the situation with deadly accuracy. "That market," he offered,
"will become crucial in the next decade. We can't afford
not to play in it."

Leonid trained that highly intelligent gaze of his on him
with an intensity that would have broken a lesser man. "We
have something in common, Harrison. My father built Siberius. It was the foundation for everything that came after
it. I *care* about the company. Maybe it's this newfound
philosophy of mine clouding my judgment. But I will *not*
sell it to you to have it dismantled in an act of vengeance."

A wave of conscience enveloped him. He pushed it
away. This deal was not about sentimentality. It was about
watching Anton Markovic shrivel up and die a slow death.
He would not allow it to be sidelined by emotion.

"This deal is not about dismantling Siberius," he said
matter-of-factly. "It's about cutting Markovic off at the
knees." If the board insisted he absorb Siberius and its
operations within Taladan and wipe out Leonid's legacy
as it surely would? Beyond his control...

Aristov turned and rested his forearms on the ledge.
"I've been thinking about what I want to be in my second
coming, Grant. For you it will be politics, I think. For me?
I've been eyeing Manhattan real estate. A couple of pent-

houses I've been looking at have come on the market and they've agreed to let me see them next week. Present me with a plan for the future of Siberius. If I like it, I'll sign it."

Harrison nodded. It would take some creative positioning but he could make it happen. "I'll have it ready."

Leonid inclined his head. His thin mouth curved in an amused smile. "What have you done to Kaminski? He was supposed to be bringing me a Frapin Cuvée."

"I had Francesca detain him."

Leonid threw back his head and laughed. "How utterly unfeeling of you, Grant."

"On whose part?"

"Why, Viktor's, of course. He is besotted."

Harrison entered the ballroom riding a heady victory that had the blood in his veins pumping in a heated rush. His head felt clearer than it had in months, his walk powerful and full of resolve as he strode through the crowd. All of the low-grade, niggling anxieties he'd harbored throughout Aristov's backpedaling lifted away like dark clouds chased away by clearer skies.

Leonid Aristov had guessed his endgame and was willing to play to make the exceedingly evil Anton Markovic pay. All that was left to do was execute. Every piece, every backdoor would be secured when Aristov signed, and the long wait would be over.

He procured a whiskey at the bar, leaned back against it and drank it down. *Congratulations to me.*

Which reminded him Francesca was likely still out there sidelining Kaminski. She'd accepted the challenge without hesitation. She had risen to the occasion. If he denied that turned him on he would be a liar. The man in him loved the fact she had the courage to stand up to him, that she wasn't afraid to tell him he was a fool. But the employer in him took his attraction to his feisty PA off the table.

He tilted the last sip of his drink toward the light and considered its amber depths. Francesca had a unique ability to read people—to draw them to her with her frank, open—charm and somehow he'd known Juliana would be no different. She had saved the day. Been his secret weapon. But he would be equally well advised to caution himself against falling under the spell of Francesca's seductive charm. It would be all too easy.

He took the last sip of the whiskey, put the glass down and went looking for his PA. Francesca might have taken on her assignment with confidence, but she was a babe in the woods when it came to dealing with men like Kaminski.

He wound his way through the throngs of people on the dance floor. It was hot and sweaty and hard to negotiate. He had just about given up on finding Francesca in the ballroom and was about to search out Juliana when he saw her on the corner of the dance floor with Kaminski.

Kaminski's hand was wrapped around her incredible body, perilously close to her bottom. Francesca had a smile on her face, but it was a hunted, close-to-the-edge smile that made a switch flick in his head. What had he been thinking?

Five long strides took him to the couple. "May I cut in?"

Kaminski gave him an annoyed look. Harrison stared back at him. Luckily Aristov's second in command wasn't a combative personality like his boss and handed Francesca over. "I'll come find you afterward," he told her with a lingering look.

No, you won't, Harrison thought. Francesca nodded to the other man with another of those smiles he knew to be plastic and stepped closer to Harrison. She stood on tiptoe. "I don't need this drink," she whispered in his ear.

The husky whisper went up his spine, then straight back down. He took the glass from her fingers, deposited it on a table and took her in his arms. She flowed easily into him without that awkwardness some women possessed, wrapping one hand around his shoulder and lacing the fingers of the other through his. "Thank God," she murmured. "I think he was about to try and kiss me again."

"He tried to *kiss* you?"

Her hand fluttered from his shoulder in a delicate wave. "My fault. On our tour of Leonid's art collection, I had to lay it on a bit thick to keep him occupied."

He frowned. "What do you mean *a bit thick*?"

"Oh, I just flirted with him…nothing *too* much, you know. It was just at one point, he said he had to go meet Leonid and I was afraid you wouldn't be finished talking so I poured it on a bit and well—maybe he sort of got the wrong idea."

Hell. "I'm sorry," he breathed. "That was my fault. I never should have sent you after him. He's clearly—" he used Leonid's word "—besotted with you."

Her cheeks went pink. "I think that's a bit of a strong word."

"I don't." He tended to agree with Leonid that Frankie had been the dangerous one in that equation. She looked stunning. He'd had to pick his jaw up off the ground when he'd seen her in that dress, not because he hadn't seen a voluptuous woman in a low cut dress before, but because on Francesca it looked like innocence and temptation personified. An irresistible combination that had had his hands itching to touch her all night.

When he had earlier on the red carpet, his palm to her beautiful back, it had been an addiction he could easily fall prey to.

He studied the high color in her cheeks, her lush, beautiful features, the spirited curve of her mouth… It wasn't just her great legs Kaminski had gone wild for. It was the whole vibrant package that made you want to be the one to capture it.

A highly inappropriate wish on his part. Which was not happening.

Her floral, feminine scent drifted into his nostrils. What was it? Orange blossoms? It infiltrated him. Attacked his common sense. It was one thing keeping his brain detached when she was ten feet away from him sitting in her office chair. Another thing entirely when she was in his arms, her ample curves tracing the length of him. She was relaxed now, lacking the tension she'd displayed earlier, her body melding perfectly with his as they moved.

She looked up at him, gray eyes tangling with his in a long, tension-filled moment where he forgot his mask entirely. The jolt of awareness in her smoky eyes marked it a huge mistake.

"Did you at least get to talk to Leonid?" Her hasty words desperately broke the spell.

He nodded. "Because of you, Leonid and I figured each other out."

"What was his issue?"

"Sentimentality. Siberius was his father's company. He's finding it hard to part with it."

"At least he's putting it in good hands…"

Guilt scored his insides. "An acquisition is an acquisition," he said roughly. "There's a lot I can't control."

"He will sign, though?"

"Yes. We need to show him a plan on how we'll assimilate Siberius into the company when he's in New York next week. But that shouldn't be a problem."

"Good, then." Her chin lifted with satisfaction. "I'm glad I could help."

"You did more than help. You were a superstar tonight. I owe you my sincere thanks."

She blinked. "Well, that's…good. You're welcome." She chewed on the side of her mouth in that anxious habit she had when something was bothering her. "I wanted to say on the plane…I mean—I'm normally a very efficient, together person, Harrison, but since I've started working with you, I haven't been myself. I've been…off. I know that and I'm not sure why."

He knew why and he wasn't going there. "Because you're still intimidated by me."

"Maybe." She nodded. "There's a bit of that…"

And a whole lot of something else. He reached his limit. "I think we should go," he announced abruptly. "Before Kaminski comes around for round two."

She nodded, her eyes on his as she stepped out of his arms. She looked as conflicted as he felt.

They said good-night to Leonid and Juliana. Leonid promised to have Tatiana call with his schedule for the following week. Viktor Kaminski looked dismayed they were leaving. Francesca stood on tiptoe and pressed a kiss to both of the Russian's cheeks. He said something to her. Francesca frowned, thought about it for a minute, then replied. Kaminski let her go.

"That was awful," she muttered, climbing into the back of the Rolls-Royce ahead of him. "He wants to take me on a tour of the Met next week when they're in town."

He peeled his gaze off her amazing rear end and got in beside her. "Tell him you're busy. You will be."

She laid her head back against the leather seat. "I will. I just feel bad about leading him on."

"He's a big boy, he'll get over it." Just like he was going to get over his intense awareness of her at the moment.

She was silent, her gray eyes contemplative. He gave the driver instructions, slid the partition closed and the car moved softly off into the night. Frankie turned and stared out at the tall, dark shadows of London as they rolled by, interspersed with bright lights. He directed his gaze the other way. She was as direct and honest as most women were deceptive and ambitious. He'd never realized what a highly attractive quality that was in a woman, when so many in his social circle made game-playing a trait acquired at birth.

Silence fell in the car. He kept his gaze trained on the skyline of London rather than on Francesca's beautiful profile cast in the light of the street lamps. The whiskey he'd consumed, the satisfaction coursing through his veins at the night's success, the attraction he'd been fighting for a week were all too potent a combination to address.

The longer he was silent, the more the tension seemed to rise in the car. Francesca stared out her window, fidgeted with her clutch strap, anything but address it. Finally he felt the heat of her gaze on him. "Harrison?"

He turned to look at her.

"Have I done something wrong?"

He frowned. "No. Why?"

Her gaze fell away from his. "I—I don't know. I feel like I've done everything right tonight and something still feels wrong."

The shadows carved the enticing hollow between her breasts in the low-cut dress. The pout in her amazing mouth had lust snagging at his throat. "There's no issue," he assured her roughly. "I told you, you were perfect tonight."

"Then why have you been ignoring me since we walked off the dance floor? Did I say something wrong to Leonid or Juliana?"

"No." He wanted to leave it at that, sanity told him to leave it at that, but the vulnerable look she wore tore at his insides. He exhaled deeply. "I'm keeping my distance."

That gray stare widened. Her hands fluttered uselessly to her lap. The uncivilized part of him knew he never should have looked at her.

"This attraction between you and me…" He shook his head. "It can't happen. We both know that."

She nodded. But her gaze stayed glued to his as if she

knew the train was running off the track, but was willing to risk full and complete disaster.

"Francesca…" The word was a final, husky plea for her to put some distance between them. She didn't. She moved toward him at the same time he brought her closer with a palm to the bare skin of her back. It felt even sexier than he remembered.

His fingers curved around her delicate jaw, and for the first time in as long as he could remember, he did something for the pure pleasure of it. He kissed the woman he'd been wanting to touch since the night he'd found her sitting in Tessa's chair.

Her lush mouth was every bit as sweet as it had promised it would be. Bare of the lipstick so many women slathered on, her lips were soft, full and edible. He took them in a slow, sensual tasting designed to entice. A soft sigh left her lips as she moved into the kiss, her hands fluttering to his shoulders. The dominant male in him liked her acquiescence. He tugged at her luscious lower lip, sucked it inside of his mouth and savored it. She tasted of innocence and sensuality all at the same time.

He waited, nibbling and tugging on her lip until her response demanded more. She angled her mouth, sought deeper contact and he gave it to her with a rush of satisfaction, slanting his mouth across hers in a kiss that didn't tease, but delivered. He didn't stop until he'd explored every inch of her mouth, drew her out of her inexperienced hesitation until their mouths were sliding hotly against one another.

His body temperature spiked. He couldn't remember the last time he'd felt so…*lost.*

Her innocence should have stopped him. Instead it obliterated his common sense. The palm he held to the small of her back pressed harder, invited her to come closer. She came willingly, her fingers curving around his bicep this time. His hand slipped to the nape of her neck, holding her still as he rocked his parted mouth over hers to request entry. Her lips parted. She tasted of fruit and wild roses. He thought for a moment that might just be *her*, but it was the champagne he was tasting, sweet and inebriating as it combined with the whiskey in his mouth.

He slid his tongue into her warmth to savor her more. Her response was tentative at first, then bolder, meeting the long, lazy stroke of his. When she'd mastered that, he probed deeper, tangling his tongue with hers in the most intimate of kisses. Her quick intake of breath hardened every muscle in his body.

He could take more. So much more... He wanted his fantasy.

That brought him tumbling back to reality. He pulled his mouth from hers and set her away from him with hands that weren't quite steady. His breathing sounded fractured, rough in the silent confines of the car.

The dazed look on Francesca's face turned to horror. "That was my fault," he growled. "Not yours."

She shook her head, her fingers moving to her lips. "I—ah—I was just as much a part of that as you were."

Maybe true, but he was the one in authority here. He had no business *indulging* himself. Being reckless at the most important crossroads of his life. With an *employee* at that. *What the hell was wrong with him?*

He ran a hand through his hair. His brain worked quickly to defuse the situation. "It's been quite a night for both of us," he said slowly. "I think we can agree that was a mistake. A brief lapse of sanity."

Francesca's head bobbed up and down. "Absolutely. It was..." Her voice trailed off, a frown furrowing her brow. "Inappropriate. In every aspect. It will never happen again."

"Good." He rested his gaze on her face. "Tonight you

proved what a valuable asset you are to me, Francesca. You went above and beyond the call of duty. I'm going to need that from you and more over the next few months… It's not going to be easy and sometimes I'm going to be a son of a bitch. But I guarantee if you stick with me you will learn more in six months than you would in six years working for someone else."

A determined light flickered in her gray eyes. "I can be brilliant for you, Harrison, I promise."

"I know that. We make a good team." So no more of *that*.

She bit her lip and nodded. The car traversed the final couple of side streets to the hotel and slid to a halt in front of the Chatsfield. He got out, helped Francesca from the car and ignored the electricity still buzzing between them. It was easy for him to cut off his emotions, what little he had. Francesca, on the other hand, was obviously still processing what had happened as they rode the lift to their suite. He could read it in the myriad of emotions flickering in her gray eyes.

He said good-night to her at the door to her bedroom. She echoed his words, walked through it and closed the thick slab of wood with a soft click. He paused for a moment when he didn't hear her footsteps walking away on the marble. Instinctively he knew she was on the other side of the door, back pressed to the frame. Thinking.

"Forget the kiss, Francesca," he said. "It was nothing."

"It's already forgotten."

Her muffled response from directly behind the door made his mouth curve. Better to put that one to bed entirely. He'd almost capped a hugely successful evening with a mistake that would have cost him dearly. Cost him his focus. And he couldn't allow that. The end was in sight. Time to focus on the master plan.

CHAPTER SEVEN

FRANKIE SPENT THE weekend replanting the flower boxes on her terrace with miniature roses, having brunch with her roommate, Josephine, and generally attempting to restore some sanity to her brain after having *kissed her boss*. She almost would have believed the party at Leonid Aristov's house had been a bizarre and unreal dream that could never have actually happened, except she knew for a fact it *had* happened when at 10:00 a.m. on Monday morning two dozen *full-size* white roses landed on her desk with a card from Viktor Kaminski.

Apparently he didn't intend to take no for an answer. *Allow me to take a treasure to see the treasures of the Met*, the card said. *Friday night? Viktor.*

She winced at the corny line. She'd told Viktor her schedule was impossible this week. She was just going to have to stick to that. And she really *was* too busy. The stack of work she had on her desk was monumental. She was going to have *no* life for the next six months.

The sweet smell of the dove-white blooms filled her nose. A wave of longing settled over her. She would die to receive roses from a man she really liked. Instead, they were from Viktor and she'd kissed her boss.

Stupid. Stupid. Stupid. Just when she'd proven she was a *valuable asset*, she'd gone and done that. She had to wonder if her mind *was* off if she was doing things like this.

She stared grumpily at her favorite flower. The fact that *Harrison Grant*, her stern, sometimes scary, stunningly attractive boss was attracted to her, was irrelevant. As he'd said, the kiss meant *nothing. Except*, it had been the most sensational experience of her life. It was one thing to feel chemistry with another person every time you were in the same room together. Another thing entirely to *feast* on it.

Her email pinged. The report she needed from marketing had come in. Josh was coming up to discuss it with her. *Good.* She could definitely use the distraction.

By the time Harrison strolled into the office late afternoon looking every inch the automotive magnate he was in a light gray suit and a white shirt that showed off the color he'd acquired sailing with a business acquaintance on the weekend, she'd made a significant stab at the outline of the Aristov plan.

He shot a pointed look at the flowers. "Don't tell me... Viktor."

She nodded.

He shook his head. "Best to give him the permanent brush-off this time."

"I know. I really wish I didn't have to do it in person."

His mouth quirked. "Oh, come now, Francesca. The art of a good brush-off is an excellent skill to have as a young woman in New York City."

She put her pencil down. "I can't imagine you've ever been on the receiving end of one. I wouldn't think it's very nice."

"The point isn't to be nice. That's what gets you kissed in elevators."

She was considering a clever response when he grabbed the card from the flowers and scanned it. She held out her hand. "Give that back."

He waved it at her. "It's in Russian. What did he say?"

Heat filled her cheeks. "It's a private note."

His ebony gaze sat on her face. "My principled Francesca," he murmured sardonically. "I would expect no less from you. Do you want me to talk to him?"

"*Absolutely not.* I'll handle it."

"Fine." He nodded toward his office. "I need to make a couple of calls then we can start on the plan for Leonid."

"I'm almost done the outline." She glanced at her watch. "It's almost five. Should I order dinner in?"

He flexed his shoulders and frowned. "I've been inside all day. It's gorgeous out there. Why don't we do the work on my terrace and my housekeeper will make us dinner?"

She wasn't at all sure putting them on anything but a business footing was a wise move at this tenuous stage, but she wasn't about to stir the waters of what seemed like an inordinately sunny Harrison day either.

"Sounds good," she agreed. "It'll be much nicer to get out of the office."

He finished up his calls, they collected their work and drove to his penthouse on Central Park West in Harrison's elegant Jaguar. His penthouse was located on the top level of the coveted Central Park West address that everyone who was anyone seemed to be bickering over, but few were lucky enough to obtain. It was beautifully decorated, of course, customized by Harrison's architect during construction so that an entire grand staircase had been moved to one end to create a wide-open floor-to-ceiling-window-lit main level that accommodated his art collection.

Done in sleek, bold colors, with blue and slate dominating, the penthouse reminded her of his office. Sterile and unobjectionable. She slipped her shoes off and wandered over to survey the art. It was not a collection on the scale of Leonid's—maybe twelve pieces in total, but priceless no doubt from Harrison's four-million-dollar Chagall purchase. She walked from one to the next, remembering Viktor's sermon about what to look out for. When she reached a Chagall done in the same vibrant blues as the one Harrison had bought in London, she stopped and took it in. They could be from the same collection.

"It'll have company now..." She jumped when Harrison spoke from behind her. He moved with a catlike grace that made him virtually undetectable.

"Relax," he drawled, his mouth tilting with amusement. "I'm not Viktor Kaminski."

No, he wasn't. He was far more dangerous. Especially when he smiled like that. It was like watching the sun come out on a rainy day. She shifted her gaze back to the painting to get her pulse under control. A bird and a woman were perched in a magnificently colored bouquet of flowers floating over the waters of what must be Nice, with its palm trees and similarity to the one she'd seen in London. Again, as with the other one, the image did not make complete sense. The bouquet had the tails of a fish instead of stems, and the buildings dotting the Riviera were curved not straight.

"It's fantastical, almost supernatural," she murmured. "Things that shouldn't be together are and it seems perfectly natural. Like he envisioned some sort of alternate universe."

He nodded, his gaze moving to the painting. "I think he did. The art historians describe his work as figurative and narrative art. Chagall was embraced by many—the surrealists, the cubists, the suprematists—but he rejected them all. He created a new reality for himself—one that was based on both his inner and outer worlds—the story, the dream he wanted to tell. This series in Nice," he said, waving a hand at the painting, "is always very mystical and inspirational. The colors are incredible."

She got that completely. "Is he one of your favorites?"

"Likely my favorite." The amber flecks in his eyes she found so fascinating glimmered in the expertly angled lighting, giving him a softer appearance. "Some of his later works are much more heartbreaking. They speak of the personal tragedies he suffered before he ended up here in New York."

"I would like to see some of those. I'm sure they'd be amazing."

"They are very moving."

She found herself fascinated by this side of him. The emotion in his eyes when he talked about the artist hinted at a depth to him, an ability to feel he kept hidden underneath the layers.

He read her expression. "You're surprised." His lips curled. "The beast does feel, Francesca. When he lets himself."

*Like that night in the car...*when he'd let go of that formidable control of his and kissed her senseless.

She couldn't help taking a step on the dangerous side. "Why doesn't he let himself do that all the time?"

He lifted a shoulder. "A beast doesn't need to connect. He lives on another level entirely."

That he did. Her mouth pursed with the desire to speak, but she shut it down. He might tell himself that. But everyone needed to connect, to experience their human ability to feel. Even a beast.

"Shall we get started, then?"

He nodded. "Elisa is making a shrimp-and-lobster paella. Would you like a drink first?"

She shook her head. "Mineral water is fine." Tonight she was keeping this all about business. Every last single minute of it.

The pentagon-shaped terrace, boasting coveted southern, eastern and western views of New York, including one of Central Park, was an amazing space to work in.

Frankie booted up her PC in one of the comfortable seating areas scattered around the space, and took in the view.

"I've received input from Marketing and Sales," she told Harrison when he returned with their drinks.

"Good." He came over to sit beside her to look at the screen. He was overwhelmingly male and distracting with his long legs splayed out in front of him. It was going to take all her powers of concentration to keep her mind where it should be.

"Did we get operations to mock up an organizational structure?"

"Yes, it's here." She flipped to the slide. The drawing illustrated every division of the massive company that was Grant International, including a new parallel subcompany to Taladan for gauges and meters in Siberius. It was mind-numbing to look at, the scale was so vast. Pretty much every piece of a car you *didn't* see on the outside was made by Grant International.

Harrison studied the diagram. "That's fine. Slot an overall positioning slide in at the beginning and I'll give you some points."

She added an up-front slide. He started dictating points, then stopped, backtracked and changed some of his wording. It sounded like semantics to her but she kept typing.

"Point three—the Siberius brand will be maintained as is, pending the outcome of the operations group and consumer research studies."

Frankie started typing. He frowned and waved a hand at her. "Delete that. I want to bury it further down in the plan."

Bury it? Why would they do that?

She kept her mouth shut. He had a reason for everything he did, much of it unbeknownst to her. They finished the opening slides and started on the marketing plan. Frankie thought the team had done an excellent job of making gauges and meters a sexy topic for the industry audience the campaign would be targeted at, but Harrison ripped out two of her favorite ideas.

"Why?" she asked, with her newly granted ability to question. "Those are really smart, creative ideas that work for the target audience. Isn't that key to growing a brand?"

He nodded, his dark lashes coming down to veil his gaze. "But I think it's overkill in this case."

They moved on to the next section of ideas the marketing team had grouped as "core must-haves." The first point included ads in trade publications. "Take that out," Harrison instructed. Now she really didn't understand. When Josh had gone through the ideas with her he had told her advertising was key to creating mass awareness for a product. "If nobody in the North American market *knows* about Siberius's cool products," she asked, "how are you going to expand its base?"

He gave her a pained look. "Expanding Siberius's base isn't an important priority for us right now. It's doing fine in the strength areas it currently occupies."

This was hurting her brain. She put her laptop down and eyed him contemplatively. "Correct me if I'm wrong, but aren't we supposed to be *selling* Leonid on how Siberius will flourish within Grant International? Encouraging him we are the right way to go? He said he had innovative products no one else has. How do we promote those?"

"Every company *says* they have innovative products," he bit out impatiently. "I am conscious of not setting unrealistic expectations when anything could happen when the board gets ahold of this deal."

She frowned. "But of course they'll support the plan if this is the only way you can get Leonid to sign. They'll have no choice."

"That's an idealistic way to look at it, but the reality is they'll do what makes business sense. *I* can only make suggestions. In scenarios like this when we're acquiring similar resources, the board will likely force us to streamline the two companies into one. It's doubtful Siberius will be left standing as its former entity."

"So why are we spending all this time doing a plan?" The words were hardly out of her mouth before it hit her. Harrison had no intention of keeping Siberius intact. He was going to lure Leonid in with this plan and dismantle Siberius when it was done.

Every bone in her body hated the idea. The company had belonged to Leonid's father. He wanted his legacy preserved. That had been his whole hesitation in signing.

She eyed him. "It's a bait and switch."

The impatience in his gaze devolved into a dark storm brewing. "No," he rejected in a lethally quiet voice. "I made a promise to Leonid to do what I can to see Siberius preserved. It is beyond my or any other CEO's control to promise him it will remain intact when business realities say it won't."

Yet he wasn't even giving the company a fighting chance with this plan. She lifted her chin. "I see."

"Francesca…"

She shook her head. This was the part where she needed to stop talking because it got her into trouble. "Let's keep going," she said quietly, looking down at her screen. "Where were we?"

"Francesca," he growled. "This is business. Put the self-righteous look away and be a big girl. You have no idea of the stakes here."

The "big girl" remark did it for her. She looked up at him, eyes spitting fire. "Dictate to me what you want in this plan and I will do it. But do not ask me to say that this is right."

"It *is* right." His ebony gaze sat on her with furious heat. "This is the law of the jungle. Only the fittest survive."

"In your world," she said evenly. "Not in mine."

"And what would your world have me do? Allow some other predator to snap Siberius up because I'm the one *stupid* enough to tell Leonid the truth? Not happening."

"I believe in karma," Frankie said stubbornly. "I know what a good man Leonid is. He's putting his trust in you."

The fury in his eyes channeled into a livid black heat that was so focused, so intense, it scorched her skin. "I know all about karma, Francesca. I know more about it than you will ever want to know in your lifetime. Trust me on that."

She watched with apprehensive eyes as he got up, paced to the railing and looked out at the fading light of New York. Having him ten feet away allowed her to pull in some air and compose herself. This job meant everything to her; she was proving she could make it on her own. But so did the principles upon which she'd been brought up.

"I'm not trying to be difficult," she said quietly to his back. "But my father taught me to treasure my ethics at all costs. That if I was ever in a situation that would make it hard for me to sleep at night, maybe I shouldn't be a part of it."

He turned around, leaned back against the railing and rested his elbows on it. His anger had shifted into a cold, hard nothingness that was possibly even more disconcerting than the fury.

The chill directed itself her way. "Although my grandfather built Grant Industries, it was my father who had the foresight and brilliance to modernize its methods and transform Grant from a successful but stagnant regional player in the American auto industry to a force to be reckoned with worldwide. He spent every minute of his life at the office, sacrificed *everything* for the company and eventually it paid off. When I was ten, my father came home one night with a big smile on his face and told us Grant Industries had made the list of the one hundred most profitable companies in America." He lifted a brow. "Imagine. Coburn and I were only eight and ten—but we got that, we got what that meant."

She nodded. Wondered why he was telling her this.

"As soon as we finished university, Coburn and I joined the business. It was in our blood just like it was in our father's. We had the bug. But neither of us ever expected to take on the mantle so soon."

Because his father had killed himself.

Her insides knotted, a cold, hard ball at the core of her. The skin on his face stretched taut across his aristocratic cheekbones, a blank expression filling his eyes. "One day my father's usual superhuman working day stretched into two. Then three. He looked like a wreck. He would go into the office, put his engineering teams through crazy all-night sessions, then come home and sleep it off. At first we weren't too concerned—it wasn't unlike him to be tunnel-visioned when he was working on a project. But the pattern started getting more and more frequent. More dramatic. One particular night, he came home and he was talking so fast none of us could understand him. We couldn't get him to rest so we called a doctor. He was diagnosed that night as a manic depressive."

Her heart went into free fall. "How old were you?"

"Fifteen."

"Oh, Harrison." She went to get up but he held out a hand, staying her.

"His condition got progressively worse as the years went on. The stress of success and the accompanying pressure made the cycles more acute, sent him into longer bouts of mania. My mother had to focus entirely on keeping him well and ensuring his condition was kept under wraps so the press, the shareholders, didn't catch on."

To the detriment of her boys' emotional well-being.

"We thought we had his condition under control after

handling it for two decades. Then my father made a deal with Anton Markovic to buy one of his Russian-based companies."

Anton Markovic? The sadistic oligarch Juliana didn't like in her house?

For the first time since he'd starting speaking, a flare of emotion moved through his dark gaze. "My father saw the potential in a post-Communist era and knew it would only grow. Buying Markovic's company was supposed to cement Grant as the most powerful auto parts manufacturer in the world. Except Markovic sold us a false-bottomed company that was on the verge of bankruptcy. Under normal circumstances, Grant would have easily absorbed the hit but we were overexposed at the time, in the midst of leveraging capital for an expansion. As a result, the debt from the deal almost crippled us."

She tried to absorb all the information he was throwing at her. "Couldn't you have gone to the courts?"

"We did. His holding company was bankrupt by then."

She swallowed hard, not sure she wanted to know where the story went after this. The emotion in his eyes became hard to watch. "Coburn and I told him it'd be fine. We'd rebuild ourselves stronger than ever. But the miscue threw him into a depressive state he couldn't pull himself out of. There was also the stress of his impending race for governor of New York." His lashes swept down over his cheeks. "My mother left the house for a half hour one day, thinking he was asleep. I came home to find he'd shot himself."

Oh, my God. Her heart broke into a million pieces. It was public knowledge that Clifford Grant had shot himself at the family residence. *But to find your father like that, by yourself?* This time she did get up and walked over to him, setting her hand on his bicep.

"I am so sorry, Harrison."

He looked down at her hand as if it was an intrusive appendage that had crept into his lair and threatened his solitary confinement. She could feel the emotion he declared he didn't have vibrating through him. Then his eyes hardened until they resembled an exotic, impenetrable rock, polished by the elements he'd endured until there were no cracks, no dents, just icy determination. "I'm not looking for your *pity*, Francesca. I told you this because I need you at my side with this deal. I need you to *understand* where *I'm* coming from. Acquiring Siberius is the final piece in my plan to cut Anton Markovic off at the knees for what he did to my father. The company is valuable to me only because it supplies Markovic with vital instruments."

Understanding dawned. Suddenly all of it—Harrison, Coburn, the way they both were—it all made sense. Coburn spent his days running from the truth, Harrison pursuing vengeance.

He wanted her on board so he could land this deal and finish Markovic. Collateral damage in Leonid was inconsequential.

"So we finish the presentation, he signs and it's done. What does this have to do with me?"

His expression was implacable. "I need you to be a part of this until he signs. Leonid likes you. Kaminski likes you. You will smooth out the rough edges."

She turned to look out at the park. It was lit by the skyscrapers surrounding it, a beautiful oasis in a cutthroat city of deal makers. It wasn't lost on her that Leonid was a cutthroat businessman himself who undoubtedly had his share of blood on his hands. No one in a position of power could avoid the gray areas. It was the gray that defined you.

But it was the emotion she'd just seen in Harrison's eyes that clutched at her heart. A raw incomplete grief that was as present now as it had been when Anton Markovic had torn out his heart.

Dampness attacked the corners of her eyes. She blinked

it back and did what her father had always taught her to do. She went with her gut. And perhaps a large slice of emotion. Because no human being should ever have to go through what Harrison had without making it right.

She turned to him and nodded. "Let's get back to work, then."

His gaze darkened. "I'm an honorable man, Francesca. I will keep my promise to Leonid if I can. But it will ultimately be up to the board."

She hoped he could. But sometimes a need for vengeance could wreak havoc on such honor.

CHAPTER EIGHT

HARRISON WAS HAVING trouble sleeping. Dawn was breaking across Manhattan, a vibrant ribbon of burnt orange stretching low across the skyline, casting the base of the skyscrapers in a mist of shimmering fire. It mirrored the turmoil inside of him, the slow burn that threatened to engulf him.

He'd had maybe three, four restless hours of unconsciousness before he'd abandoned his bed and greeted the morning. There was too much on his brain, too much to accomplish, too many decisions that impacted too many people.

He watched the sun, a bright ball of fire, penetrate the mist and make its way into the sky. Today was the day Leonid Aristov would either cement or destroy his seven-year plan to wipe Anton Markovic's empire from the face of the earth. To do that, he must stretch the truth, make a man believe something that was quite likely not possible.

It was eating at him. Plaguing him. He grimaced and set his elbows on the smooth limestone ledge that bounded the terrace. At thirty-three his conscience was making an unexpected appearance and he had little difficulty wondering why. *Francesca.* His personal moral compass who sat on his shoulder, reminding him that the world was not black and white. That one wrong did not right another.

Except in this case it did. Leonid would lose his legacy regardless of who bought Siberius. And he would never let Anton Markovic get away with what he'd done.

He frowned into the hazy pink, orange light. Francesca, on the other hand, was a gray area he couldn't seem to control. A woman unafraid to call him on who he was. The woman whose kiss had woken up something inside of him he'd thought long ago dead…

He didn't let himself think of Susanna, ever, because he'd done what he'd had to do in the months following his father's death. He'd compartmentalized his emotions until there was only rebuilding his father's legacy left, cutting out the rest, including his longtime girlfriend. It had been an act of survival for a twenty-five-year-old who'd lost his mentor and couldn't afford to lose everything else.

Susanna, a smart, young financial broker, hadn't been content to live her life with a shell of a man. And who could blame her? When he'd finally come to terms with his father's death, she'd moved on, found someone who was more "emotionally available." It hadn't just been the last few months, she'd told him sadly, it had been her battle over their entire relationship to get him to open up. "It's never going to happen, Harrison. I give and you take. I need more."

His fingertips dug into the cool stone. He hadn't told Susanna he'd been breaking apart inside, that he didn't know how to let the pain out, because he was inherently flawed by his experiences. He was better off on his own. And his descent into the world of the unfeeling had worked just fine until Francesca Masseria had roared into his life and stamped her do-gooder presence all over his psyche.

He raked a hand through his spiky, disheveled hair and frowned. So that kiss had reminded him he knew how to feel. That he didn't have the emotional IQ of zero his brother thought he had. She was his employee. She was too innocent for a jaded animal like him and she was messing with his head.

If that wasn't enough, he had her tied up in knots over her ethical quandaries. Plenty of reasons to stay away.

The sun rose higher between the buildings, insistently making its presence known to the Manhattan morning. His anxiety rose with it. The political bloodhounds chasing him had stepped up their campaign. Wanted a decision. It made his head want to blow off. To mount an independent run for the presidency meant walking away from Grant. It meant altering his life in a way he could never take back. How could he possibly make such a decision *now* when all he could see was a marker on Anton Markovic's back?

A fatalistic curve twisted his lips. Some would see such ungratefulness at so much opportunity as foolish. Yet it had never been his idea to get into politics. His grandfather had been a congressman. His father had wanted to be governor. Yes, he saw a need for change, but was he the man to do it? Or was he too much of a rebel to make it work?

When his head got too heavy to sit on his shoulders, when he thought it might actually blow off, he headed for the gym. When he got into the office at six-thirty, Coburn was already there.

His brow lifted. "Time change got you?"

"Brutal. But the blondes were fantastic."

He shook his head. His brother had been in Germany for the past week meeting with the manufacturers who built their automobiles with Grant parts. "Try being a little less predictable," he taunted, setting his briefcase down on Coburn's desk.

"I dunno," Coburn came back thoughtfully, tossing his pen on the desk. "I think you're holding your end of the stick surprisingly well lately. You have the political pundits on the edge of their seat."

"Because they have nothing interesting to talk about."

Coburn leaned back in his chair. "Are you going to do it?"

"You'll know when I do."

"Right." His brother's gaze narrowed. "And then there were the photos of you on the red carpet with Frankie in London. When did you start taking your PA to social events?"

"Since she spoke Russian."

"That was quite the dress she had on."

He recognized his brother's predatory look. "She looked beautiful."

"She was a goddamned knockout. But you, H?" His brother lifted a brow. "Haven't seen that sparkle in your eyes in years. Sure you haven't caught the Frankie bug?"

"She was useful, Coburn. That's all."

"I think," his brother ventured thoughtfully, his magnetic blue eyes lighting up, "we should invite her to the Long Island party. She can wear that dress."

"*Francesca?* I don't think that's a good idea."

"Why not?" Coburn challenged. "She's good enough to take to a million-dollar Aristov party, but not good enough to mingle with your Yale friends?"

His brows came together. "This has nothing to do with class. Frankie is an employee."

"You invited Tessa last year."

"Because she'd worked with me for two years."

Because he hadn't wanted to put his hands all over his married assistant...

"I'm going to invite her," Coburn announced definitively. "She's *my* employee and she deserves to come."

He crossed his arms over his chest. "Don't you think she's going to feel out of place with all those people she doesn't know?"

His brother shrugged. "She can come with me."

A discomforting feeling speared his insides. "*You* don't have a date?"

Coburn spread his hands wide. "Dry. Completely dry. I can make sure Frankie has a good time."

He didn't like that idea *at all*. "You said you were going to stay away from her."

"I intend to. But that doesn't mean she doesn't deserve to come." Coburn pursed his lips, his gaze moving over his brother. "Unless you want to take her. Or are you escorting the poor, neglected Cecily?"

"I haven't seen Cecily in months."

"Like I said—" Coburn winced "—poor Cecily. Anyway, Mother would like to know if you're bringing a date."

He was sure she would. It was only then that he realized the party was next week. "I'll invite Francesca," he rasped. "You inviting her would give her the wrong idea. I can position it as a job well done."

"Fine. Aristov sign?"

"Today's the day." He borrowed a page from Francesca's book of optimism. He needed it. Badly.

Frankie took one look at a beautiful, Tom Ford–suited Harrison as he walked into the office and knew she'd never seen him wound so tight.

"Good morning," she said carefully. "Coffee?"

He gave her a distracted look. "Sorry?"

"Did you want some coffee?"

"Oh…yes. Stronger the better, thanks."

She decided that might not be a good idea. She made the cup half strength and carried it into him.

He took a sip. Frowned. "It doesn't taste strong."

"It's strong." She gave the bags under his eyes a critical look. The man didn't sleep. But she was not his mother.

"Tom Dennison called a few minutes ago. He says you haven't responded about the fund-raiser."

Harrison scowled, fatigue creasing the lines of his face. "Tell him I'm in China."

She gave him an even look. Tom Dennison was one of the most powerful businessmen in America, the CEO of a consumer packaged-goods company as well as a highly political animal who liked to shake things up.

"I'll tell him you're occupied with the shareholder meetings," she suggested instead. "And ask him to please send over the details again so you can get back to him tomorrow."

"Brilliant." Sarcasm dripped from his voice.

Leonid better sign tonight. It was her only hope. She took a deep breath. "Have you eaten breakfast?"

"No, thanks."

"I'll get you some granola and yogurt at the deli."

"Francesca," he growled but she was already out the door.

Things went from bad to worse. Leonid's meeting with the penthouse developers was delayed by three hours while he waited to get the paperwork done to buy. Harrison fumed that the Russian clearly didn't have his priorities in order if a penthouse was more important than a *forty-million-dollar deal*. "*Everything* is always more important than a forty-million-dollar deal."

Now Aristov and Kaminski weren't going to be available until after six and Leonid had suggested they meet at the vodka club he frequented for drinks instead.

"How are we supposed to finalize a deal at a *vodka club*?" Harrison snapped.

"Sealing a deal over a meal or drinks is becoming more commonplace in Russian culture," Frankie soothed. "Take a deep breath."

He glared at her from across the desk. "I am not six, Francesca."

Right now you are. Her eyes must have said what her

lips wouldn't because his stare turned positively lethal. *I would prove it to you*, he threw back, *if we didn't have a moratorium in place. But since we do, you are out of luck.*

The electricity simmered and crackled between them. Francesca sucked in a deep breath of her own before it exploded. "I will print copies of the plan to take with us. Anything else we need?"

Closure, his gaze fizzled.

She turned and walked out of his office, heart slamming in her chest.

Leonid's vodka bar was in the heart of Manhattan at Broadway and West Fifty-Second Street. The VIP room the owner directed them to was one of the most unique spaces Frankie had ever seen. A huge cathedral-shaped stained-glass window glowing with a rainbow array of colors that graduated from blue to pink to yellow was the focal point of the room. Green-and-gold wainscoted walls were accented by a vibrant patterned wallpaper in the same colors that climbed up and over the ceiling. A rich, ornate carpet in complementary tones claimed the floor while two stunning chandeliers bookended the room.

She couldn't decide if she loved it or if it was just much too much. "Certainly more interesting than a conference room," she told Leonid as he gave her a kiss on both cheeks.

"I thought so."

Having obtained two of the penthouses he'd had his eye on under fierce competition, Leonid insisted they begin with a celebratory drink. They toasted the deal with vodka that surprisingly didn't taste like rubbing alcohol, but like absolutely nothing instead. Thus the potency, she warned herself.

After a few minutes of real-estate chatter, Harrison went through the plan, his jaw set, expression intent. Leonid stalled at the piece about an operational study of Siberius determining its internal and external positioning within Grant Industries. "You told me Siberius will remain a distinct brand. This makes it sound like it's up in the air."

Harrison regarded him evenly. "I cannot promise you the board will allow me to preserve Siberius's separate identity, Leonid. You know as well as I do these decisions are made with the numbers in mind. I will, however, influence the process as much as I can. But I cannot lead you on and say it's a given."

The room went so silent, so fast, Frankie could hear the ultraquiet fans in the ceiling whirling. Harrison's face was utterly expressionless. Leonid sat watching him, his shrewd eyes assessing. The Russian's fingers ceased their tapping on the table. Frankie's heart stopped in her chest as he placed both palms on the edge. *Was he going to leave?*

After a long moment, Leonid looked at Harrison, his mouth set in a grim line.

"Thank you for being honest with me."

Harrison nodded. Frankie exhaled.

"Continue, please."

Harrison went through the remainder of the plan. It was stripped down, basic and promised very little. When they got to the end, Leonid gave it a long look, flipped it over and threw it into the middle of the table. "Not much there to get excited about."

Harrison eyed him with that deadly, combustive look he'd been carrying all day. "I would say forty million dollars is a great deal to get excited about. As far as a second coming, it's a very nice start."

The Russian was silent. He stood up abruptly, pushing his chair back from the table. "Give me a few minutes. I need some air."

Viktor Kaminski raised a brow as his boss walked out of the room. Harrison's face grew so tight she thought it might snap in half. Since he was like a live bomb right now and she didn't want to encourage Viktor further, she excused herself, saying she needed the ladies' room.

The patio and some air beckoned instead. She stepped out onto it. No wonder Leonid had needed air. He and Harrison had been sucking the room dry since they'd stepped into it.

The patio was packed with people enjoying the steamy summer night. The smell of lilac came from the tree flowering in the garden. Lazy jazz floated on the air from the club next door. Francesca walked to the edge of the garden and stood drinking it in. She wasn't sure when Leonid appeared beside her, tall, thin and contemplative as he smoked a cigarette.

"Don't tell me it's bad for my health." He read her disapproval. "It's one of my few real vices."

"I won't, then."

His eyes glittered with amusement. "I like that about you. This honesty you have. If you don't say it, you can read it in your eyes."

"It's a curse." Her mouth twisted. "Ever since childhood. It got me in a lot of trouble."

"So it is."

He was silent, puffing elegantly on the cigarette. When he finished it he tossed it to the ground and snuffed it out under his foot. "Should I sign it?"

Her breath caught in her throat. "Sign what?"

He turned that hard, whiskey-colored gaze on her. "The deal. Should I sign it? Is Grant the honorable man I think him to be?"

The world closed in around her, the chatter of the crowd, the croon of the music melding together to create a buzz in her ears that seemed deafening. She didn't want to be any part of this. She'd never wanted to be any part of this. And maybe that was what Leonid had sensed.

If she balked now, she would ruin Harrison.

She pulled in a breath, conscious of the Russian's gaze on her face. And said the only thing her conscience would allow. "He's a good man. I wouldn't work for him if I didn't think so."

He watched her. Evaluated her. It was like being inspected by a customs official, the intensity of it. Then he nodded, an expression she couldn't read passing through those cat's eyes of his.

"*Harasho*. Let's go inside, then."

Harrison watched Francesca and Leonid walk back into the room together. Her face was white and pinched, tension stitching her delicate features together. It made the tiny hairs on the back of his neck stand up straight.

Leonid, on the other hand, looked focused and alert. He sat down at the table and signaled for another round of vodka. Harrison's heart pounded in his chest, drowning out everything but what was about to happen. Seven years of waiting and planning could not end in anything but success.

He sat there in agony while Kaminski engaged in small talk with Francesca as they waited for the vodka. The server came back laden with a tray of four glasses. He passed them out. Leonid lifted his glass. "Right, then," he said, looking at Harrison. "We have a deal."

Relief slackened every muscle in Harrison's body. His heart slowed its frantic pace. *It was done.* The last piece was in place. The crystal tumbler felt heavy in his hand as he raised it, eyes on Leonid. "We have a deal."

The vodka slid down his throat and warmed his insides. He had expected a surge of victory. For everything to feel *right* for the first time since he'd started this quest. Instead he felt nothing. Nothing at all except a numbness, an absence of feeling that was almost frightening in its intensity.

He distracted himself by glancing at Francesca. Her long lashes swept down over her cheeks as she took a sip of the vodka then pushed the glass away. Whatever had gone on outside had rattled her. Even in his distracted state, the glitter in her gray eyes burrowed itself beneath his skin. What had gone on between her and Leonid?

They finished the vodka. Leonid requested a fully executable contract be sent to his lawyer the following morning. If he got the green light that Harrison was sure he would because the lawyers had already scoured the document, he would sign.

He kept waiting for the euphoria to hit him. While he smiled at Leonid's joke about missing their personal chess matches each day. As they said goodbye to the two men and climbed into the car, Francesca stopping to speak to Viktor. While he stared out at a now dark New York. It never came. Why wasn't he on top of the world? Why didn't the victory feel sweet instead of bittersweet? He could close in on Anton Markovic now and bring it all full circle. Make him understand his pain. Wasn't that what he'd always wanted?

It made no sense.

He glanced at Francesca. The pinched look hadn't left her face. If anything it was worse. "Did you let him down easy?"

She turned a conflicted gaze on him. "I told him I was hung up on someone else. It seemed nicer to do it that way."

He wondered if she meant him. He could not deny he was more than a little hung up on her. And fighting it bitterly.

Her gaze fell away from his. He rested his head against the back of the seat. "What did Leonid say to you outside?"

Her mouth pressed into a straight line. "He asked me if he should sign the deal. If you were the honorable man he thought you were."

His head came off the seat. Her gaze moved back to his, stark and most definitely under siege. *Aristov had asked her that?*

"What did you say?"

"I said you were a good man. That I wouldn't be working for you if you weren't."

It had cost her integrity a great deal to say that knowing the scenario he'd painted. He closed his hand over the fist she had curled on the seat. "Thank you."

Her gaze dropped to his hand. "It's the truth. You are a good man."

With a cross to bear she didn't agree with... His hand remained closed over her fist. He fought the desire to bring it to his mouth, to press his lips to her skin until she released the tension and he could taste the salt on her skin. He wanted her. He wanted her so badly he could taste her already under his mouth. But she was unavailable to him.

He released her hand before he did it. His skin pulsed with the need for more because that touch, *her touch*, was the only thing making him feel alive right now.

He brought his back teeth together. Fought it. Recited to himself all the reasons he couldn't have her. *Good* reasons.

Derrick slid the partition open and asked, "Where first?"

He gave him Francesca's address.

She shook her head. "We're closer to you. I need the papers for the Detroit project to work on while you're out in the morning. I'll come up, get them, then Derrick can drive me home."

It made sense. It would also get him out of this car sooner. "Fine. That works."

Derrick stopped in the circular driveway at the side of the building. They rode the elevator to the penthouse in silence, neither of them about to address the tension and push things over the edge.

He found the papers she needed on the desk in his study and carried them out to the living room. "Text me if you need any clarification." The delicate fingers he'd just held closed around them. Her gaze fastened on his, probing, seeking. "I'll see you tomorrow afternoon then."

"Yes." He willed her out of the apartment with a curt, dismissive look. He needed to be alone or he needed to drown himself in her, but he couldn't do anything in between.

She was halfway to the door when she stopped and turned around. "Harrison, are you okay?"

"I'm fine. Thank you for your help today."

She nodded and left. When the door closed behind her and he heard the sound of the elevator whishing its way toward ground level, he poured himself a drink he knew he didn't need and took it out onto the terrace. The moon was a perfect, giant orb in a sheet of black. Luminous; full of promise. It should have been another signpost of where he was headed. Vengeance. Yet he continued to feel nothing. The fear he dreaded always found a way in, insidious as it was, worming its way into his consciousness.

He lifted his palms to his temples. Willed it away. It was nights like this, nights when he scaled Mount Everest and won, when any other human being would have been basking in the glory, that he wondered if the darkness would claim him, too.

There had never been any sign he had picked up his father's genetic markers for mania, but the depression beckoned, whispering along the edges of his mind. He raised his eyes to the Grant tower, a shining beacon of what made America great. Had his father known how close to the flame he was flying? Or had he been blinded by the heights he ached to achieve?

Would it be too much for *him*? His head pounded with

the weight of too many decisions. Too many paths that were no longer clear. *Too much, too much.*

A jet banked over the Hudson, the lights on its wings flashing in the darkness. He stared at it, hypnotized by the pulsing flares. *Is destiny the fate of every man? Is your path irreversible no matter how you pursue it? Or is there a way to rise above it? A way to blaze a path that is yours and yours alone?*

The throbbing in his head intensified. He needed to escape, but he didn't know how.

CHAPTER NINE

FRANKIE COULDN'T GET into the car. The haunted, hunted look on Harrison's face when she'd left, the way he'd been ever since Leonid had agreed to sign the deal, was gnawing at her. She'd expected him to be victorious and superior. Instead she'd found him dark and introspective.

Working nearly 24/7 with someone meant you were in tune with their moods, and the Harrison she'd witnessed tonight was one she hadn't seen before. One that scared her. Leonid might have passed it off as exhaustion, distraction, but she knew it was much more.

Derrick gave her a quelling look. He wanted to get home to his family. He thought she was nuts standing here on the sidewalk, utterly caught in limbo.

She got into the car. They pulled smoothly away from the sidewalk, weaving into traffic. Her stomach churned in big, conflicted circles. She had led Leonid to believe he could depend on Harrison when in reality he would likely be bitterly disappointed. Whether Leonid had read between the lines or taken her words at face value was something she would never know.

A soft curse left her lips. She didn't want anyone's future revolving around her. Then to make her choice only to have Harrison turn into a stone wall when he had been handed everything he'd wanted? *What is going on?*

She clenched her hand into a fist and pressed it against the seat. Was he feeling guilty for what he was about to do to Leonid even though he'd laid his cards on the table? Or had he finally realized, with the final piece in place to destroy Anton Markovic, that vengeance was a poor substitute for a broken heart? That it would never bring his father back?

Or was it something else entirely? That call from Tom Dennison today? The twisting in her gut intensified. She couldn't do it.

She tapped on the screen. Derrick opened it. 'Yes, ma'am?"

"Can you take me back? I've forgotten something."

He gave her a supremely patient look. "Of course. Let me just find somewhere to turn around."

When he deposited her on the sidewalk outside Harrison's building once more, she thanked him and told him to go home. "I may be a while."

Derrick nodded. "Call me if you change your mind."

She was out of her mind. Setting her jaw, she entered the building through the side entrance. The door required a thumb scan to get in but Harrison had taken care of that for her last week when she'd had to come collect some documents for him. She rode the whisper-quiet elevator to the penthouse, heart pounding in her ears.

The doors of the elevator swished open. The apartment was eerily silent as she moved through the entrance way and into the living room. The precious artwork glowed silently on its perfect cream backdrop. No Harrison.

His study was in darkness. A glow from the terrace suggested he was there. She walked through the living room and stepped outside. Harrison was standing at the railing, looking out at the skyline. Her heels clicked on the concrete as she walked toward him. He turned around, frowning. "Did I forget to give you something?"

"No." Her knees betrayed just the slightest wobble as she took the last few steps toward him. "I just—" Her voice trailed off. Just what? What the heck was she doing here?

She came to a stop in front of him. Her gaze rose to his. He was as tall and commanding as ever, as stomach-clenchingly beautiful, but the tormented look dominated now. It emanated from every pore of him, blanketing her in his desperation. She pulled in a breath.

"I wanted to make sure you were okay."

The shadows in his face darkened. "I told you I was fine. Go home, Francesca."

"But you aren't." The words spilled from her mouth. "Ever since Leonid agreed to the deal, you've been off."

"I'm *fine*."

She frowned. "It's what we've been working toward. I thought you would be happy."

"I *am* happy." The emotion vibrating in his voice sent a shiver down her spine. He turned to look at the skyline again. "It's none of your concern, Francesca. Go home. I'll see you in the afternoon."

She stood her ground, legs shaking now. For a man who claimed to feel little emotion it was written in every taut muscle of his body. In the rigid column of his back, his neck. In the barely leashed confusion that surrounded him. It reached out and wrapped itself around her, pulling her toward him.

"Sometimes," she said quietly, laying a hand on his arm, "the things we want the most, the things we think are going to make us feel better, don't. *Can't* because they were never the solution in the first place."

He spun to face her, dislodging her hand. Antagonism poured off him in waves. "Nailing Anton Markovic to the ground is going to make me feel better, Francesca. *Much better*. Make no mistake about it."

Her heart thudded against her rib cage. "Then why? Why are you like this?"

"Because I have too much going on in my head." He practically yelled the words at her. "This is not another case of you saving the day, Francesca. It's far more complex than one of your little sermons can fix."

Her stomach lurched. "I didn't suggest that."

His mouth curled. *"Go."*

"I won't leave you like this."

The deliberate way he looked at her made her pulse buzz in her ears. "You would be very wise to do so," he suggested in a low, deep voice that made her insides liquefy. He lifted a finger and dragged it across her cheek, watching as she shivered in reaction. "Otherwise I will do what I was aching to do in the car and drown myself in *this*. And I think we've both agreed it's an unacceptable result."

His touch felt like fire on her skin. The kiss from London sizzled through her head, beckoning her on to sure destruction. They were like hot and cold fronts converging in a storm it seemed impossible to outrun.

But he was her boss. She loved her job. She really must go.

He slid his thumb down to her lips, his gaze holding hers as he traced the trembling outline of her mouth. *"Go,* Francesca. You're the only thing making me feel alive right now. If you don't, I can't be responsible for what happens next."

Run, her sensible side commanded, hurting man or not. But the other side of her, the one pulsing with an awareness of him so strong it made her mouth dry, wanted him to drown himself in her. Wanted to experience that type of passion. Because *he* made her feel more alive than she'd ever felt in her life. Being the center of his attention was *hypnotizing.*

The tremor in his hand as he stroked the pad of his

thumb over her bottom lip made her heart turn over. She couldn't go.

His dark gaze glittered. *"Out. Now."*

"No."

The word hung on the air between them, defiant and crystal clear. She watched the control fizzle in his eyes at the same time he reached for her hand and brought it to his mouth. He pressed his lips to her palm in an openmouthed kiss, as if tasting her very essence. Her pulse ran wild.

"You have five seconds to leave," he murmured. "Or you *don't.*"

She closed her eyes as he pressed another kiss to her palm. Counted out the seconds in her head. His soft curse split the night air.

"Francesca."

She brought his hand to her mouth. Found his palm with her lips. *He* tasted hot, salty and hedonistically male. She wondered if he'd experienced the same stomach-churning intensity of it. The way he went completely still said he might have.

He let her play for a while, to know him. Then he curled his fingers around her wrist and brought her the two steps forward he needed to let her feel the heat his tall frame emanated.

"You're sure?"

She nodded. His fiery, conflicted gaze scoured her face. "I won't take an innocent."

"I'm not." She didn't need to tell him there had only ever been one, awkward and disappointing as the sex had been.

The warm night air heated up around them, like it was catching fire, too. He slid his fingers into her French twist and started pulling pins out. The buzz in her ears was so loud she couldn't hear them hit the concrete, one by one. She should have been terrified with what little she had to bring to this insanity. Instead she trusted him on a level she didn't understand.

He pulled out the final pin. Her hair fell loose around her shoulders. He lifted a hand and fingered a silky strand, a curious look on his face.

"What?"

"I can't figure you out," he murmured. "Honest, fearless, unsure of yourself at times yet so sure of so many things on a bigger life level." He wrapped a chunk of her hair around his finger and let it slide through his hand. "It's why Leonid asked you that question tonight. Because the essence of you is good. It emanates from you."

Her lips pursed. "It's the way I was brought up. I don't know any different."

"I do." He bent his head and put his mouth to the hollow between her neck and shoulder. "You don't seem real to me."

She wasn't sure if that was a good or bad thing. But then it didn't matter as she abandoned herself to the sensations his lips were evoking on her skin, the warm slide of his mouth across her heated flesh sending sparks to every inch of her body. He savored the hollow he'd found, pulled every reaction out of her with his lips and teeth. The arch of her neck, her soft sighs, guided him. *More.* He set his hand to her jaw, moved it to the other side and did the same masterful job to the matching sweet spot between her left shoulder and neck. It made her weak in the knees. She curled her fingers into his waist and anchored herself to him.

He slid his hand to her nape and took her mouth then. Hot, possessive and never-ending, it wasn't like his kiss in the car. It promised carnal, exciting things to come and it made her rational brain shut down.

He pushed her jacket off her shoulders and threw it over the railing. Dispensed with the buttons on her blouse so expertly it made her wonder what the heck she was doing, thinking she could play in Harrison's sandbox. By the time he'd undone the last button and bared her to his gaze, her cheeks were scarlet. The look of pure lust that crossed his face sent that thought flying off into the nether.

"You are so beautiful," he murmured, absorbing her with his eyes. "I swear to God I thought you were an apparition the night I walked into the office and you were sitting in Tessa's chair."

She bit her lip. Remembered her complete mortification. How shameless she must have looked, her skirt riding up her thighs, her lace stockings on display...

"Oh, yes." His gaze was on her face. "I had dreams about those. That and the handcuffs... They did me in."

She covered her cheeks with her hands. He shook his head and pulled them away. "It was the sexiest thing I've ever seen..."

Her heart beat a wild rhythm in her chest. The decadent, openmouthed kiss he pressed against her lips almost felled her unsteady legs. The thought she could never sit in that chair again without blushing, that *this* would change *everything*, crossed her mind as his palms closed over the weight of her breasts and his thumbs slid across her hardened nipples. "Don't," he growled in her ear as she stiffened beneath him. *"Not tonight. Feel."*

She obeyed his command, because even in her inexperience, she knew only Harrison could ever make her feel like this. It had been that way from the beginning.

The pleasure he was lavishing on her as he rolled her nipples between his fingers with both hands unearthed a low moan from her throat. Sharp, urgent need lanced through her, sending her fingers to his biceps to curl into taut, hard male muscle. He rewarded her by sinking his teeth into her shoulder in a gentle bite that promised more was coming. *Much more.*

Oh, lord. She was so, so out of her depth.

His knee nudged her legs apart. She anchored her palms against his chest as he ran his hands up the back of her thighs. She had left the lace stockings off for an entire week after the *incident*, she'd been so mortified. But habit was habit and she loved feeling feminine. His swift intake of breath when he found the lace edging reverberated through her head. "You're killing me."

He slid an arm under her knees and picked her up. She had a vague memory of him doing that that night on the plane, but she'd been half unconscious then. Now she was fully alert, fully aware of the power caged in his muscular frame. Her heart raced in her chest, slamming against its containing walls. He was insanely strong. She had handed herself over to him to do what he liked. It inspired a feeling of mild panic.

He nudged the French doors shut behind them and carried her through the dimly lit penthouse and down a dark hallway toward the bedrooms. His was the big master suite at the side of the apartment. Her heart reached up to tattoo itself against her eardrums as he set her down in the middle of the lushly carpeted floor and switched on a lamp. She distracted herself with the jaw-dropping view of Central Park while he stripped off his tie and tugged his shirt collar open with a sense of purpose that made her heart stutter. Digging her toes into the plush carpet, she avoided the urge to turn and run out the door of his very expensive penthouse.

The deliberate way he moved back toward her almost rattled her poise completely. It must have shown on her face because he stopped in front of her, captured her hand and lavished another of those erotic, tongue-infused kisses to her palm. "Trust me."

Everything inside her melted. Her gaze fused with his dark, tormented one. "I do."

He curled her fingers around the top button of his shirt. She latched on to the direction like a lifeline, slipping the buttons free with hands that shook slightly but managed the job in a far less efficient process than his had. When she had them undone, he yanked the shirt from his trousers and threw it to the floor. He had the most amazing chest she'd ever seen on a man. She rocked back on her heels to take him in. Hard, muscled, honed by the hours he put in at the gym every week, he was the most perfect example of masculinity she'd ever seen. It was almost intimidating to touch him, but she couldn't help herself. Her hands moved by instinct, sliding up and over him, wanting to learn every inch with this liberty she'd been given.

Everything about him was impenetrable, indestructible, except tonight his vulnerability allowed her a way in. *It was intoxicating.*

She slid her palms over his nipples. He tensed under her touch but held himself still. Fascinated by how rock hard the hair-roughened peaks were underneath her fingertips, like tiny pebbles, she explored them with the pads of her thumbs.

He groaned. "More."

She wasn't sure what he meant until he covered her hand with his and slid it down over his trousers. The scalding contact with the hard, thick length of him made the blood roar in her head. Eyes closed, she traced him, learned him. He leaned into her caress, his growl sliding into a velvety moan of approval. It made her feel empowered, emboldened. She stroked him more firmly, pressed her palm against the impressive bulge of him and felt him grow harder beneath her touch.

His palms returned to her thighs, sliding up the back of them. This time he slipped his fingers beneath the lace and caressed the ultrasensitive skin there with fingers that burned her skin. "These stay on."

Frankie forgot her task completely as the raspy timbre of his voice shot through her. He slid his palms higher until he reached her lacy panties. Her hands fell to her sides, her head dropping to his chest as he nudged her legs apart with his knee, moved his fingers beneath the lace and touched her so intimately her back arched in pleasure.

"Harrison." His name slid from her lips on a groan of pure pleasure. He repeated the caress again, his fingers sliding against her slick skin. Leisurely at first, he stroked her like he might a cat, caressing her nerve endings. Then he deepened it, intensified it. She let him take her weight as her knees buckled. His voice was a husky demand in her ear asking if she liked it. Commanding her to tell him when she wanted more. She did because this was beyond anything she'd ever experienced, it felt that good.

His hands left her aching flesh. She wanted to scream greedily that it wasn't enough, beg for more, because she'd never experienced the type of pleasure he was giving her. But he was disposing with his trousers, intent on another kind of pleasure entirely. He slid off his briefs and kicked them aside. Her mouth went dry, her palms sweaty. She could have expected he'd be big because of his size but his arousal, proud and daunting, kicked her heart into a whole other gear.

He was as aroused by her as she was by him.

He pushed her blouse off her shoulders, found the back button of her skirt and undid it. She swallowed hard to inject some saliva into her mouth as her zipper went the way of her button and he nudged the skirt off her hips. Self-consciousness would have overwhelmed her then, as she stood there only in her lacy underwear, if she hadn't been utterly fascinated by the ruddy color staining his cheekbones. The tortured look was gone. Urgent, compulsive desire was plastered across his face. He was totally and utterly fixated on her, as if he couldn't believe she *was* real.

Her gaze tracked him as he backed up and sat down on the bed. He pulled a foil package from the night table drawer and rolled a condom on his impressive erection. She watched him, finding his beautiful body such a turn-on it was impossible to look away. His gaze lifted to hers when he'd finished, his eyes telling her exactly where she was supposed to be. She moved to mere inches in front of him.

"In my fantasy you had me in handcuffs." His hot gaze singed her from head to toe. "But you didn't need them, you had me totally under your control."

Her legs felt as though she'd done a seven-hour shift at Masserias. He reached up, slid his fingers in the sides of her panties and stripped them off. She almost lost her footing when he moved his hand between her thighs and cupped her aching center. Squeezed. It was a blatant act of ownership that made her stomach dip. Sent her fingers clutching the hard muscles of his shoulders for support.

"I'm not averse to a woman tying me up," he continued, easing his grip on her to fill her with a long finger instead. "But then you wouldn't get this. And I want you as hot and wild for me as you were in my fantasy."

Frankie closed her eyes at the seductive heat in his voice. It raked over her nerve endings and sent warmth flooding to the very place he was caressing. She couldn't help her response, couldn't help moving her hips against his hand every time he filled her. It was *incredible*.

He added another of those amazing fingers, palming the soft flesh of her buttocks with his free hand to hold her where he wanted her. A low moan escaped her lips.

"That's right," he murmured, spreading the fingers he had inside of her to maximize her pleasure. *To ready her.* "That's exactly how you were."

He withdrew from her. Left her hot and aching again, but only to shift both his hands to the backs of her thighs and lift her on top of him. She wrapped her legs around his waist, her thighs making contact with his hot, aroused body. Too many contact points fried her nerve endings. The unleashed power of him beneath her made her pulse speed up into an almost impossible awareness of his masculinity. But most intense of all were his eyes. Dark and full of want, she felt him all the way inside of her.

"You do something to me," he rasped. "I can't explain it."

She couldn't, either, but she felt it, too. She watched the desperation flicker back to life in his eyes as he fought it, fought the physical and mental connection they shared. The lack of control…it was a last-ditch effort to hold on to the darkness and she wouldn't allow it. She brought her mouth down on his in a kiss so intimate, so soul-consuming, she was sure she would never forget it.

His hands bit into her bottom as he lifted her up and brought her down on the hard column of flesh that telegraphed his desire for her.

"Tell me," he muttered against her lips, "if I'm hurting you…"

But he had brought her to the edge, to a greedy, grasping place where he was all she wanted. Inside of her. *Exactly like his fantasy.* Her body was malleable, soft as she accepted the tip of him. He was big; he stole her breath as he brought her down on him with firm hands. It was a tight, exquisite fit, one she almost couldn't stand. But when he had filled her completely, she wanted more.

"*Then what did I do? In your fantasy…?*" she whispered.

He took the weight of her hips in his hands, his eyes locked on hers. "You rode me like an angel."

Oh. She went down then, lost in the way he made her feel. She circled her hips around him. Took him deep inside, then retreated. His eyes caught fire. His hands helped her move. Then there was nothing between them except the sensation of being impaled on him. She took him again and again until her body was all soft heat, grasping him, *needing* him.

It was unmistakable, the sweet intensity that built inside of her then as his size, his girth touched a spot that promised heaven. She gripped his shoulders harder. He slid a hand between them and rubbed his thumb against her center. Back and forth in a path of fire that had her limbs clenching around him. "Give yourself to me," he commanded roughly.

She closed her eyes. Let his thumb take her over the edge. Her back arched, white lights exploded in her head as an orgasm racked through her. Her gasp as it tore into the night was raw and pleasure-soaked. Animalistic.

It was hot and amazing and never-ending. When she finally came down. Harrison was watching her, a deadly heat in his eyes. Her lashes lowered. "Don't," he commanded, his thumb claiming the curve of her lip. "You were spectacular."

She opened her eyes. Allowed him to part her mouth with his thumb, her breath coming hot and hard against his skin. She could taste herself on him. Taste what he'd done to her. It was too much. *Overload.*

He rolled onto his back and took her with him. He was buried deep inside of her, pulsing and rock-hard. *Unsatisfied.* His gaze morphed into the darkest, deepest granite as it ate her up. He wanted her to blow his mind. To obliterate his thoughts.

She leaned forward, pressed her palms to his chest and rotated her hips in a slow, grinding circle. His hands tightened around the flesh of her bottom. Faster, harder, he urged her down on him until his eyes were glazed and she knew he had lost it completely. But she drew it out, knew he wanted her to. He drove up into her with awe-inspiring stamina, again and again, his erection sending sparks of aftershocks through her. Slowly, amazingly, she felt her pleasure build again, hovering over the edge of another sweet surge of heaven. This was why he'd made it last. Because he could give her this.

He read the tautness of her body, his face blanking as he took her hard and fast, fully in control now. *"Again."*

She gave herself into the deep, piercing release, lost to him as he came with a hoarse shout, his hips bucking against her. Aftershocks jerked his powerful body. They racked through her as she dropped her head to his chest and tasted the salt of his skin. Nothing had ever felt so right. So perfect.

And yet it was so wrong. The cool night air sent reality flickering across her sweat-dampened skin. He was her boss. At least her temporary boss. And she'd just had scorching, wild sex with him.

Harrison rolled her beneath him, his big body holding her captive. His gaze found hers. Narrowed. "Stop thinking."

"I can't think," she muttered. "My brain is mush."

"Good." He left the bed, disposed of the condom and came back to her, hooking a finger under the front closure of her lacy black bra. "How did this stay on?"

Her cheeks flamed. Because they'd been in such a hurry?

He lowered himself back onto the bed beside her. Her cheeks heated as she absorbed his magnificence. It was a bit overwhelming. Dark amusement gleamed in his eyes as he captured one of her hands, pressed his thumb to her palm and worked the tension from it.

"It bothered you to say that to Leonid tonight…"

She closed her eyes as the magical pressure of his fingers made her tingle right down to her toes. "Not because I don't think you're a good man. You are. It's what happens to Leonid's legacy that I have an issue with. You tearing his company apart like that… My family has owned Masserias for thirty years. If someone bought them out and changed everything I'd be brokenhearted."

He pressed his thumb into the joint between her thumb and forefinger. Frankie almost moaned out loud. *"So why didn't you go into the family business if you love it so much?"*

"My parents wanted me to. *I* wanted to forge my own path. I've wanted to work as a PA for as long as I can remember. I always thought it was so glamorous, but challenging at the same time."

"Glamorous? With a tyrant like me?"

She opened her eyes. *"You* are a different case."

His gaze darkened with intent. "Okay," she admitted, "I love working with you when you're not in one of your moods. You have an amazing brain."

He grabbed her other hand and started working on it. "Only my brain?"

"And the rest of you…" she conceded. "I appreciated all of you from the beginning, much to my dismay. That is so utterly unlike me."

"You had a thing for my brother…"

She gave her head a shake. "Why do you keep saying that? Coburn is attractive and charming and I like working for him, but I've never had a *thing* for him."

"You idol-worship him."

His tone was decisive. She put a hand on his chest and levered herself up to look at him. "My lord, you Grants have the biggest egos. I do *not* idol-worship Coburn. He is an inspiring, wonderful person to work for. He treats me like I'm an equal, valued partner. A somebody…but that's it."

He frowned. "Of course you're a somebody. You're excellent at your job."

She glowed at his praise. Harrison meant every word he said. "I was a disaster with you at first."

"Because your mind was in the gutter. Exactly where mine was."

The warmth in her cheeks intensified. "Sometimes you need validation," she told him. "My parents didn't think a career was the right place for me. I never had a good GPA. It was average, if that. They thought I should be managing Masserias because I'm so good with people." Her mouth curved. "My dad says I have the magic touch."

"You certainly do."

The meaningful tone in his voice made her swat him. "Harrison."

He unsnapped her bra. She arched away from the mattress to allow him to strip it off, although that proved to be a bad idea because the slide of his fingers over the bare curve of her breast, over its taut center, were infinitely distracting.

"What about your brothers and sisters? Did they go into the family business?"

"I have five." Her mouth twisted in a wry smile. "One's a neurosurgeon, one's a psychologist, then there's the chemical engineer, banker and if you like the nontraditional route, my brother Salvatore is an entrepreneur with a state-wide series of fitness clubs at twenty-six."

"The one who forgot the cake?"

She nodded. "So you can see why I was the obvious choice to take over Masserias... The unspectacular one of the bunch."

His chin lowered. "I think that's an inaccurate description. You handle people with a deftness I've rarely experienced, Francesca. You have great natural instincts for business and you speak three languages."

So did her sister Federica: English, Italian and Spanish. *And* she was a psychologist.

She gave him a pained look. "You don't need to try and make me feel better. I'm at peace with who I am."

"Are you?" She didn't like how his far too perceptive gaze seemed to look right through her. "You should shift some of your absolute truths into the department governing your opinion of yourself. Ten minutes with Juliana and she's explaining the psychology of Leonid to you. That's a *gift*."

"Speaking of Leonid," she offered casually, "care to talk about what's making your head too full?"

His eyes flashed. "No, in fact."

The intimacy of their position, the way the hard muscles of his stomach quivered as she traced her way down toward the sexy dip between his abs and leg spurred her to dig a bit more. "Could you put up enough of a stink with the board that they would maintain Siberius as a separate entity? Keeping in mind, of course, we're only talking in hypotheticals."

His gaze narrowed. "Perhaps. But when you only have so much political capital with a board, you choose your battles wisely."

"Right." She left that hanging in the air between them because she wanted him to think about it.

"Francesca," he growled. "Stop meddling."

She followed the sexy dip down over his muscled thigh, luxuriating in the hard, densely packed muscle beneath her fingertips. "Juliana says Anton Markovic is an evil man. That he has underworld connections that make her wish Leonid didn't do business with him." She looked up at him. "Does he know you're after him?"

"No." He captured her exploring hand in his. "And you can put his name out of your head. Juliana's right. Anton Markovic is not a man to be played with."

"Yet you are…"

"*Francesca.*" He bent his head and put his mouth to the curve of her breast. "I think I'm going to have to silence you."

That might be fine, too. His mouth closed over her hardened nipple, scoring it with his teeth. The way he used those sharp incisors was truly…remarkable. A moan broke from her throat. "That is not fair."

He drew her nipple into his mouth with a hard suction that made her whole body go rigid. The slide of his hairroughened leg as it parted hers rendered her distraction complete. He really *wasn't* finished with her.

She moved against him, her smooth legs luxuriating in the feel of his harder male limbs. His teeth and lips teased her other nipple into a hard, aching button. It took him about five seconds to drag her back into the maelstrom.

"Now we go freestyle."

Freestyle? Oh, the fantasy. That was apparently over and they were onto a very vivid, very real exploration of her stomach. The tender, vulnerable skin of her lower abdomen… She clutched his coarse hair in her fingers. He couldn't do *that. Not after what they'd just done.*

She tugged on his hair. "Harrison." He made a low sound in his throat and nudged her tensed legs apart. She jammed her eyes shut as his fingers parted her and he slid his tongue against her slick flesh. The way he savored the essence of them was too intimate. Too much. But then again everything about tonight had been too much.

He rasped his approval as her legs fell open and she surrendered completely. His licks turned long and languorous, intent on waking her body up. Then they became purposeful, *unrelenting.* He waited until her limbs stiffened, she dug her hands in his hair and came, shuddering against his mouth before he moved his way back up her body, slid another condom on and took her with a deep, breath-stealing thrust. She threw back her head and reveled in his possession. In the hot, sweet perfection they made together.

When he sought his release with a ragged groan and buried his mouth in her throat, she held him to her while the storm they had created together unleashed its final fury. His breathing slowed, evened out. It was long minutes before she levered herself up onto her elbows and saw that he'd passed out in her arms.

A primal instinct, a need to nurture, stirred deep inside her. It was stronger than the magnitude of what she'd done with her career tonight. Stronger than all of it. Because in that moment, she knew no matter what the morning brought, *this* had been right. She had pulled him back from the edge.

If it had also tipped her feelings for him, a man she could never have, into dangerous territory? If her own emotions were wildly out of control? That was the stuff of tomorrow.

CHAPTER TEN

IT WAS THE LONG, elegant leg thrown over his that convinced Harrison something was very off in his universe. The floral perfume hit him next...heady and distracting. It occurred to him he might be having another of his very inappropriate dreams about his PA and he latched on to the desperate appeal of that thought with gusto. He opened one eye to verify. No, he was not dreaming and yes, that was Francesca sprawled on top of him, the tantalizing floral scent of her mixed with something that could only be described as steamy hot sex.

That she'd had *with* him in *this* bed *last* night.

Mother of God.

He closed his eyes. Traced the steps back in his head. Leonid had agreed to sign the deal and for some bizarre reason instead of feeling elated, he'd felt curiously dead about it inside. The darkness had descended to take the place of the numbness, the monsters in his head had roared to life and it had all become much too much.

Francesca, somehow sensing, with that bizarre intuition of hers, how low he'd sunk, had returned. At his weakest point. When he hadn't been able to do anything but take her apart like he'd wanted to for the past two weeks. He had seduced her, *drowned himself* in her. And when it was done, he'd still felt like he'd only skimmed the surface of what they were.

His hand clenched around her smooth thigh beneath his palm. Francesca murmured and moved against him. He extracted himself from her, his guts turning in a slow, discomforting twist. The intimacy they had shared had been overwhelming and unexpected. But far more damaging had been what he had revealed. The scary depths his mind could scale if he let it... The tortured part of him. The man no one knew.

A cold layer of perspiration blanketed his skin. Never did he let anyone see his vulnerabilities. His weaknesses. Yet Francesca had walked in here last night and smashed through his defenses with one sexy kiss to his palm. He shuddered to think what she'd witnessed. His was not a darkness he chose to show to anyone. And he'd been darker last night than he had in ages. Completely inside his head.

He ran a palm over his damp brow. It didn't surprise him that it had been Francesca who'd broken through to him. What shocked him was how completely he had fallen under her spell. How thoroughly she had pushed the torment away. Until there had only been the purity of her to ease his troubled soul.

And she had. He may have made a huge mistake with her, his head might still be buzzing from it, but the heaviness had lifted. The darkness had gone.

Her scent drifted to him again, evocative and oh so feminine. His body reacted immediately. You would think after not having sex for months and having her twice last night, he'd be out of gas. His body, apparently, begged to differ.

If he laid one hand on her now he was a goner. He knew that as certainly as the sun came up in the morning. His only hope was to get out of bed, shower and make a plan for how to handle this. He might then have a chance of escaping with his head intact. *Might*.

He reached down and slid her leg off his with the subtlest of movements. Francesca sighed and curled up in a ball. *Perfect.* He shifted his weight to the outside of the bed, eased himself sideways until he could throw his legs over the side. Another sigh. He looked back. Big mistake. If there had ever been an angel in his bed it was Francesca. Her long dark hair was tangled around her face, she had the body of Venus and goodness shone from her like a beacon to come to the light.

His mouth firmed. *Not a bloody chance in hell.*

He threw himself under a cold shower. He would get the contract over to Leonid this morning, the Russian would sign and he would execute his long-awaited confrontation with Anton Markovic. Markovic was making it easy on him with a planned trip to Washington to lobby the government. Except he would never be able to deliver on that contract because his supply chain was now owned by Grant Industries.

How unfortunate.

He stepped out of the shower and dried himself off. Francesca was still dead to the world when he slipped into the bedroom. He grabbed a shirt and trousers from the walk-in closet, dressed and made for the kitchen and coffee. A steaming cup of sensibility in his hand, he walked out onto the terrace and watched Manhattan stir to life. The lights had gone off in the park, the day-shift cabbies were taking over from the night shift and he could already see the powerful cars of the die-hard financial brokers on the road ready to get a jump start on the day.

A low oath escaped him. Things always looked better in the morning, but what had happened between him and Francesca last night? It had been such a huge error in judgment on his part, he couldn't even fathom it. They could not continue to work together after last night. She would be the end of him. If he'd been distracted before, he hated to think what he'd be like now knowing what it felt like to take her. To have all that sweetness and fire underneath him, begging for his possession.

It would make him crazy.

Except giving her back to Coburn also inspired that same feeling. His brother could seduce a woman without even using a tenth of his charm. But Francesca had declared herself not interested...

His mind slammed the door shut on the subject with a definitive thud. It was the right thing to do.

The fact that she was naked sprawled across Harrison Grant's bed hit Frankie before she registered he wasn't anywhere to be seen. *Thank God.* Pieces from the night before circulated through her head like the View-Master she'd had as a kid, except this show was not her favorite fairy-tale princesses, this was her and her *boss* acting out their deepest, darkest fantasies.

Oh, dear lord. Adrenaline fast-circuiting through her veins, she pushed off the massive bed, rustled around on the floor for her underwear and slid it and her dress on. Her lace stockings sat in a pile beside the bed. She picked them up and balled them up in her hands. No way was she going there today.

A covert operation to the living room turned up her purse where she'd dropped it on a chair last night. She shoved the stockings in it and went in search of her more gut-churning target. The compassion she'd been intent on honoring last night was fading fast, replaced by the utter horror of what she'd done. Yes, this might have been inevitable between them, but this was her *job*. When had she decided that was less important than mending Harrison's broken spirit?

Her teeth sank into her lip. Right around the same time he'd kissed her again. But it didn't negate the facts. She didn't for one minute think they could carry on like normal after *that*. Facing him was going to be hard enough.

She fortified herself with the thought she would do the same thing if presented with the situation all over again. Leaving a human being in agony wasn't an option. How she handled things now was.

The smell of coffee drifted through the penthouse, guiding her to the kitchen. When she didn't find Harrison there, she crossed the living room to his study. He was working, looking fresh as a daisy in a crisp shirt and pants. She winced as he looked up, his gaze moving over her tangled hair to her rumpled dress to her stockingless feet.

"I'm going to shower and change at home," she said hurriedly. "I was just coming to tell you I was leaving."

His gaze settled on her face. "Go get a cup of coffee and we'll talk first."

No. No talking. Just escape. His eyes narrowed. "Get the coffee *now*, Francesca."

The order brought his others from the night before back. Exciting, *forbidden*. She turned around abruptly and headed for the kitchen. *That* was not the way to handle this.

He had pulled his chair out from the desk and was sitting facing the sofa when she returned. She handed him a new cup of coffee, noting the look of absolute control on his face. The beast was back. *Good.* That would be helpful.

She sat down on the leather sofa, legs arranged in front of her like she was at a tea party. His gaze held hers. "We can't just avoid what happened last night."

"I know."

"It was bound to happen, we both know that."

She nodded again. Set the coffee on the table before she spilled it.

He steepled his fingers against his thigh and studied the arrangement. "I wasn't in a great place last night. My head wasn't right."

Tell her something she didn't know. "It shouldn't have happened, regardless of our chemistry. It creates real issues."

"I get that." Her words came out sharp and singed.

He looked up at her, his hard gaze softening into something more human. "It was amazing, Francesca. *You* were amazing. I—" He stopped, frowning, as if looking for exactly the right word, like a man on the witness stand. "I needed to escape. I needed to not be in my head. And you helped me do that."

So she was the nonrational choice. Fury fired her veins. She knew exactly what she'd been to him last night. She was shocked, however, by how much more she wanted him to say. How she wanted him to admit the undeniably special connection they shared. That last night had been as unforgettable as she'd thought it was. Even though she knew that was ridiculous. Harrison didn't commit. Last night had illustrated the demons that drove him—demons that had shut him down this morning.

She'd be so smart, so wise, to stay away. He was right.

"You needed to be with someone," she said quietly. "It's fine."

His gaze sharpened on the stubborn upper curve of her lip. He looked as if he was going to say something, then his mouth tightened. "We need to decide where we go from here. I don't think it's reasonable to expect us to keep working together under these circumstances. I'm going to send you back to Coburn after the Aristov deal is signed. I can use one of Tessa's replacement candidates until she's back."

Her shoulders rose. She knew it had been coming, but he threw it at her like one of the painful, ruthless decisions he made on a daily basis.

"And what will you tell Coburn?"

His jaw hardened. "I'll tell him it was a personality clash. My fault. He knows I'm a son of a bitch. It won't be hard to believe."

It wouldn't. But she wasn't sure Coburn would buy it. He knew she wasn't a quitter. He knew she would have made it work. However, right now, none of that mattered. All that mattered was getting out of here before he made her want to say something completely out of character. Something *angry*. Because although this was her fault, even though she had made her own bed, it was clear it was never going to be Harrison Grant's.

And that hurt in a way she didn't want to examine.

She lifted her chin, gray eyes clashing with black. "Are we done here? I'd like to go home and shower."

His eyes flashed. She watched him bank the heat down into that cool, calm control of his. "Two things. Can you call the agency and get the replacement candidates in for interviews next week?"

Wow, he wasn't wasting any time getting rid of her. "Of course."

"Good. I've sent a note to the lawyers telling them to forward the Aristov contract to Leonid. I may need your help this morning facilitating things while I'm in my meeting. Stay close to your phone."

When was she ever not close to her phone? She nodded and got stiffly to her feet. She was almost to the door, still full coffee cup in her hand when he spoke.

"Are you all right?"

She turned around and gave him her iciest look. "Perfectly fine. I'll see you this afternoon."

Harrison spent the rest of the morning in an industry meeting with various automotive groups from across the country, trying not to feel like the cad he was. He knew what Frankie had wanted to hear. He couldn't deny he'd felt it. He'd *told* her he'd felt it last night. *You do something to me... Give yourself to me...* But he would never admit it in the cold light of day.

He reached for his coffee cup, then shoved it away before he developed caffeine poisoning. He'd never had that kind of a connection with anyone, *ever*, not even with Susanna, whom he'd loved with what he'd later learned had been a surface, selfish kind of it. But it didn't mean he had the ability to offer Francesca anything, even once he shipped her back to Coburn. He couldn't even table the idea of an affair to see where things would go. That would only be cruel of him when he knew where it would lead. *Nowhere.*

He sat back in his chair and tried to focus on what the chairman of an industry group was saying. But his thoughts kept drifting back to the woman who had stormed his defenses. So Francesca had proven he had the ability to feel when he'd thought that emotion long ago gone. He would bolt at the first sign of commitment if they did pursue something. It was his history. Last night had been a window, not a door. He'd needed to make that clear and he had, hurtful or not.

The meeting dragged on until they broke for lunch. He headed back to Grant instead of socializing. Coburn was in his office working when he arrived. His brother gave him a careful look. "I thought I heard via the grapevine Aristov signed. Didn't you sleep well with your revenge plot wrapped up tight around you last night?"

Heat stained his cheekbones. "He signed. I'm here to talk to you about Frankie. *Francesca.*"

His brother's eyes narrowed. "Don't you dare back out of taking her to the party, H. She's looking forward to it."

Hell. He had forgotten all about the party. That was a problem.

"It isn't about that," he said roughly. "I think she should come back to work for you. Our styles are too different. It isn't working out. I'll find someone from the agency until Tessa's back."

Coburn sat back in his chair, his blue eyes spearing him. "You stood here yesterday telling me how fantastic she was in London. What's changed?"

He lifted a shoulder. "I don't want to strip the spirit out of her."

How true that was.

His brother got to his feet and walked around the desk. His usual urbane charm took on a dangerous edge. "It's funny all this would come to pass when I saw Frankie in the elevator this morning looking like crap. What the hell did you do to her, H?"

His hands curled into fists at his sides. He had not been the only adult present last night.

"I'm suggesting you take her back, Coburn." He gave his brother a cool look. "Do it. It's better for everyone."

His brother's eyes glittered with incredulity. "You have a thing going with her...I *knew it* when I saw those photos."

The accusation bounced off him like the far too late summary it was. "She's going to finish the Aristov contract with me this week and get the shareholder meetings sorted. We'll interview candidates for her replacement next week and you can have her back by the following Monday."

"Then what? You sleep with her a few times like you always do, then brush her off like lint on your sleeve? Frankie isn't one of your sophisticated, heartless types, H. You will *crush* her."

"Exactly why it's not happening." Or at least it wasn't ever happening again. "Take her back," he said roughly. "And spare me the sermon. You are one to talk."

"*I* was the one smart enough to stay away from her." His brother shook his head. "What about the party?"

His lips thinned. "I'll escort her like I said I would." He had a week before he had to figure that one out.

CHAPTER ELEVEN

"So you are alive…" Salvatore's deep baritone reached over the phone line, familiar and comforting. "I was instructed to check."

Frankie tossed her pencil on her desk and sighed. "Just. My boss is a slave driver. It's been nuts. One more week and I'm going back to work for Coburn and life will return to normal."

And why did that hurt so much to say? Was she a total glutton for punishment?

"You should come for a drink at Masserias tomorrow night. A few of us are going."

"I would love to but I am attending the Grant Long Island party."

Salvatore whistled. "Exalted company."

She chewed on her lip. "I'm not really *going* going. My boss asked me to be nice."

"Still, that's a score. Maybe you can net yourself a millionaire."

Unlikely. The only *billionaire* she wanted wasn't on the market for her.

"Who are you taking?"

Her teeth burrowed deeper into her lip. "No one. Harrison is escorting me. To be nice…like I said."

There was silence on the other end of the line. She could

hear her brother's protective instincts silently shifting into gear. "That's…interesting."

"Quit it, Salvatore. He considers it a *reward*. I promise I will come out next week."

"I'm taking that as a solid, set-in-stone kind of promise."

"You got it." She tapped her fingers on the desk, fighting the urge to confide in her closest sibling. "Look, I really should get back to work."

"Franks…" A pause. "You okay? You sound funny. I'm not far, I could drop by for coffee."

She shook her head. Then realized he couldn't see that. "Sorry, too busy. And I'm fine, really. Just tired."

Better not to tell him her problem was a man and that man was her boss. He'd be over here in ten minutes flat, Harrison on the other end of his black-belt-trained glare. Salvatore always brought out the real Frankie. The emotional side of her that right now felt curiously close to tears. She had been so happy here at Grant. Now it felt as though everything was falling apart. Coburn couldn't help but think she'd failed when she was getting shipped back to him, although he'd been seemingly thrilled at the idea. His temp was messing up his filing *and*, he'd added, she didn't bring the sunshine in with her.

Her heart sank another foot. Somehow that didn't make up for the fact that Harrison was clearly washing his hands of her, now that she'd soon cease to be useful to him, with the Aristov contract signed. The bright, shiny glow of her new life was fading fast and she didn't want any member of her family seeing her like this when they so clearly felt she belonged at Masserias.

"All right, then." She heard a horn sound in the background as Salvatore negotiated traffic. "Next week for sure or I come find you."

She hung up to find Jack Robbins, the head of Grant's legal counsel, at her desk. He eyed Harrison's closed door, dropped the Siberius contract in front of her and gave it a satisfied look. "Fully executed, sealed in stone. The bear will be happy, no?"

"No doubt."

Jack glanced at his watch. "I have a lunch meeting. Could you ask him to call me if he has any questions? It should be as discussed."

"Will do."

The lawyer made his way out the door whistling. Frankie could have used a bit of his good cheer. The past five days had been as bad as the pre-Aristov deal era. Only for a completely different reason. She and Harrison had been trying so hard to stay out of each other's way that it had become excruciatingly awkward to be anywhere near him. His curt, near polite behavior was so odd, it was disconcerting. Perhaps because when they came within five feet of each other, neither of them seemed able to keep their cool.

That's what happens when you have hot, sweaty sex with your boss. When you connect on a level that's way beyond the physical, putting your feelings in distinctly dangerous territory. You avoid.

She picked up the contract and got to her feet. She was so tired of avoiding she wanted to scream. At least when she was back with Coburn she could get back to normal. She wouldn't be dreaming about that night with Harrison. She wouldn't be wondering about her boss's every mood and she wouldn't be feeling the irresistible desire to comfort the beast even though he was making that hard. It would no longer be her job.

She headed toward his office. The worst was the party. She had to attend the damn thing with Harrison when she'd rather spend the night washing dishes at Masserias. And that was saying a lot.

He was on the phone when she knocked and entered.

She waved the contract at him. He motioned for her to stay and wrapped the call.

"That's it?"

"That's it. Fully executed and ready to go. Jack said to call if you had any questions."

"Good." He laced his fingers together and pressed them to his chest. "You've been such a huge part of this. Why don't I take you to lunch?"

Lunch? She stared at him as though he was nuts. "You have a lunch meeting."

"So I'll cancel it. You deserve some appreciation for the great job you've done."

She eyed him. *She'd done her job and this was his kiss-off lunch.* It was guilt talking. Looking at that contract in his hands, knowing what he was going to do with it, knowing thousands of people were likely going to lose their jobs when he folded Siberius into Grant made her feel *unwell.* Angry. *Used.*

"No, thank you," she said stiffly. "I appreciate the offer, but I seem to have lost my appetite today."

His black eyes glittered at her. "You okay?"

"Perfect. Would you like me to go down to the deli for you?" She gave the clock on the wall a pointed glance. "Your meeting starts in ten minutes."

"I'll get it myself afterward."

She spun on her heel and walked.

"Francesca."

She held up a hand and kept going. Last week it had been him on the edge of an explosion. This week it was *her.*

Harrison dressed for the annual Grant summer party the next evening with the grim determination of a man who'd been through the interminable small talk and politics so many times he could have run it in his head before it had even started. Divorces would be announced, affairs would surface and rumors would abound about everything from political campaigns—namely *his* or his lack of one this year—to high-profile job losses and corporate defections. The only thing that changed was the players. And sometimes, if they were misguided or unlucky enough, they stayed the same, too.

He'd been in a filthy mood ever since Francesca had walked out of his office, her back ramrod-straight, her icy look telling him exactly what she thought of him. Which was so *unfair*. They were adults, they'd done what they'd done and sulking wasn't going to help the situation.

Meanwhile, he was struggling. Did she think this was easy for him? He had done everything, *everything* to put her out of his head and move on, including setting up his "accidental" meeting with Anton Markovic with exquisite care. He had buried himself in work, used the nights to consider his future and refused to think about how much he craved Francesca's level set outside the office as much as he valued it inside.

While he attempted to deny that that night with her had changed everything.

He muttered an oath. Picking up his jacket, he rode the elevator to the parking garage and drove the short distance to Francesca's apartment on the east side.

Something inside him did a slow roll when he saw her standing on the sidewalk, glowing in a crimson-colored gown that was less body-hugging than the one she'd worn to Leonid's party, but still heart-stoppingly sexy on her hourglass figure. She was an unattainable goddess for a man still mired in his head.

He got out, walked around the car and stopped in front of her. He couldn't help taking a long look. Her hair was up, done in a million curls caught on top of her head. Sparkly earrings dangled from her perfect ears. Her feet were encased in dainty silver shoes that accentuated the arch of her delicate foot. But it was her eyes that tugged at his heart. They were a deep, unsure gray, so unlike her usual spirited self.

It was going to be a long, long night.

"Hi." His voice when it rumbled from his chest was rusty and not his own. Frankie's eyes flickered. How insanely articulate of him. That was the way to handle a tough crowd.

He cleared his throat. Took another stab at it. "You look stunning."

"Thank you." Her stiff demeanor wasn't bending one bit. *Fine.* He could play this game. He put her in the car, walked around to the other side and started driving. Relentlessly he plied her with small talk. Frankie gave one-word answers, sometimes a handful. It was a ninety-minute drive to Long Island and that got old fast. She was angry, concluded the male in him. Women didn't know how to separate the emotional from the rational while men were rarely in touch with their feelings. He wondered how it actually ever worked.

He even asked her how Tomasino and the gang were doing at the church. Instead of scoring him points, it made her mouth tighten even more. So he shut his mouth, turned on the radio and drove.

They arrived at the Grants' redbrick Georgian mansion on Long Island Sound just in time for cocktails. Dropping their bags in their rooms, he gave her a quick tour of the elegant, dark-paneled house with its checkerboard marble grand hallways and massive tapestries. He could tell instantly Frankie liked it more than his penthouse.

The minute they appeared in the back garden, his mother pounced on them, emerging from a crush of people gathered under the fairy-light-strung trees with her usual gray-haired, impeccable elegance. She had Frankie summed up in three seconds flat, her keen blue gaze slid-

ing over the brunette who bested her petite frame by a
good six inches.

"So you're the Frankie my boys are so enamored with."

Frankie blushed. "*Enamored* is hardly the word. You
have lovely sons, Mrs. Grant. I'm lucky to have my job."

"They're lucky to have you," Evelyn Grant countered
smoothly. "Every powerful man needs a supporting cast."

Harrison kept a supporting hand at Frankie's back, even
though it was clear she didn't want it there. If anyone knew
the value of a supporting cast, it was his mother. She had
been that her entire life as the matriarch of this family,
these days focusing far too much of her attention on her
sons' careers.

His mother gave him a pointed look. "Tom Dennison
was asking after you. Perhaps I can introduce Francesca
around?"

He didn't know why it bothered him to let Frankie go.
It was better that way, keeping their distance from each
other, and his mother would undoubtedly do a superb job
being the social queen that she was.

He glanced at Frankie. "Okay?"

She nodded, but he knew her well enough now to catch
the trace of trepidation in her eyes. His mother had a reputation, no doubt about it, but Frankie was more than up to
it handling her. She had no problem handling him.

He left the women and found Tom Dennison enjoying
a drink on the far end of the patio with a couple of other
power-broker CEOs. Dennison made a joke about him
being a mirage, then folded him into a tight-knit discussion of politics and current affairs. It was clear Dennison
was offering him his backing and that of his political side-
kicks if he elected to run. He kept his poker face on and
tested the waters.

His mother, true to her word, introduced Frankie around.
At some point she handed her off to Coburn, who kept her

at his side as he moved from group to group, his usual life-of-the-party self. As the night wore on, he watched Frankie's sparkle return. Her eyes glowed, and as Coburn's eligible friends flirted with her, she smiled often with that combination of shyness and pleasure he found so damn appealing.

A knot formed itself in his chest. More than a few of the single, imminently successful types seemed interested in the beautiful brunette. *And why not?* She was everything a man could ever want in a woman. Gorgeous, smart and witty. The type of girl they could put a ring on and know they were damn well lucky to have her.

He grabbed a glass of wine from a passing waiter's tray, the tightness in his chest growing. He was not those men. No man could ever really change his spots for a woman. Not even for one who'd turned his mind and body upside down in the space of a few weeks. If the darkness in him didn't destroy her, his life would. Because after he'd brought Anton Markovic to his knees, he might enter the nastiest arena of all—a place he could never imagine good-hearted, ethical Frankie in.

Hors d'oeuvres were served and the champagne flowed. The four-piece band who'd been playing the Grant party for almost two decades struck up a tune. He had just extricated himself from a long discussion with one of his father's oldest friends when Cecily Hargrove found him in all her bubbly blond enthusiasm.

"Harrison," she admonished, giving him a kiss on the cheek. "You didn't return my phone call."

When had that been?

"A month ago," Cecily clarified, shaking her head at him. "Daddy is a workaholic, but you are worse."

He studied her with fresh eyes, this socialite from a family so connected she could ease the way for a presidential run in multiple eastern states. Perfectly straight hair with clever highlights, big blue eyes and a stick-thin figure that wore clothes perfectly, she did nothing for him. She would make the ideal wife for a governing official. She would never say the wrong thing, she would never counsel him to be anything he wasn't or question his intentions.

She would never make him feel as alive as Frankie did.

"Let's dance," Cecily insisted, tugging on his arm. "I've just been horsing in Montana. I have to tell you all about it. The skies were amazing."

Frankie watched Harrison escort a beautiful, petite blonde onto the dance floor set among the twinkling fairy lights. It was like a dagger to her heart watching him emerge from his political networking only to immerse himself in the blonde. *Which was nuts.* They didn't have anything according to Harrison. She was better off paying attention to one of the good-looking men chasing her who actually might send her roses. Who might not kick her out the morning after as if she was a piece of unwanted furniture.

She could not, however, contain her feminine curiosity. "Who is that?" she asked Coburn, posing the question with the casual air of someone who'd just spotted a nice-looking car and wondered what brand it was.

"Cecily Hargrove." Coburn made a face. "I'm surprised it took her this long. She's usually on him like paint."

If Frankie's mood could have sunk even lower, it did. The woman Harrison was supposed to marry, according to the oddsmakers. She was *perfect.*

Coburn's eyes went a mischievous, vibrant blue. "Want to have some fun?"

She forced a smile to her lips. "I am having fun."

"I mean some *real* fun." He grabbed her hand and started walking toward the dance floor, a series of flag-stones set under the trees. "Play along with me."

Doing what?

Coburn took her in his arms on the dance floor, where the band was playing a Frank Sinatra classic. At least she didn't feel so barefoot watching Harrison dance with Cecily when she was in the arms of handsome Coburn. He was a great dancer, better than Harrison, his smooth lead easy to follow. It would have been lovely, enjoyable if she didn't have to watch Cecily smiling up at the man she was obviously crazy about.

She averted her eyes and focused on what Coburn was saying. Another song started. Everyone stayed on the dance floor. Coburn pulled her closer. She looked up at him, startled. "Relax," he murmured. "I'm having some fun with my brother."

The glitter in his eyes made her wince. He knew. She'd been sure he was smart enough to figure out what had happened between her and Harrison, but the verification was mortifying. *Oh, lord.*

She thought about denying it, then sighed. "He isn't going to care. Forget it."

"You don't think so?" Coburn's gaze was pure wickedness. "Give me five minutes."

Frankie started to protest. Then defiance kicked in. *Pride.* When Coburn pulled her into a closer hold, his cheek against hers, she let him. His hand moved to the small of her back, his lips to her jaw. The couple beside them gave them an interested look.

"Coburn…"

"Wait."

The band belted out the high notes of the sultry Ella Fitzgerald classic. A dark shadow fell over them. Coburn lifted his lips from her jaw as if pulled from a particularly delicious moment. "H?"

She turned her head. Harrison stood beside them, Cecily Hargrove in tow, a dark cloud on his face. "My turn, I think. We should switch."

Coburn didn't release her right away. The stare between the two brothers dragged on. Cecily bit her lip and stood there watching. "Only," Coburn murmured finally, releasing her, "if you bring her right back."

"Not bloody likely."

Frankie's head spun as Harrison took her hand and pulled her into his arms. Coburn did the same with a bewildered Cecily. Her new partner did not have the same smooth rhythm as her previous one. His steps were forced and jerky. *Angry?*

She looked up at him. "Harrison, what's going on?"

"I could ask you that." His voice was clipped, ruddy color striping his cheekbones. She stared at him, about to confess Coburn had been having some fun with him. The words died in her throat.

"I was simply dancing with Coburn."

"He was *kissing* you."

"Oh, not really," she denied. "What does it matter anyway? You've made it clear we aren't going to pursue what's between us. I'm a free agent."

"So you move from *one brother to another*? I thought you had better morals than that, Frankie."

He was calling her Frankie. He was also jealous. Extremely jealous. The knowledge hit her like a ten-table arrival on a busy Masserias Saturday night.

The opportunity to make him admit his feelings was too tempting to resist.

"Maybe I'm taking your advice. After all, I was a big mistake. You said it yourself."

A lethal glimmer stoked the heat in his eyes. "I was trying to be *smart* for the both of us."

"Fine. Take me back to Coburn. Go dance with Cecily. It's probably for the best."

The heat in his gaze overflowed. She watched it unleash itself, swirl through the air like a wisp of smoke coming off a fire. His hand tightened around hers, just short of making her yelp as he turned and headed off the dance floor, dragging her behind him. She half ran to keep up, Coburn watching the whole thing with an amused, satisfied look on his face.

"What are you doing?" She dug her heels into the grass when they'd cleared the dance floor and pulled to a halt.

He gave her a hard look. "We are going to the boathouse to talk. The only place no one will be. You want to walk or do I carry you?"

Her heart tripped over itself. She wasn't sure she wanted to be alone with him like this. And he would not do that. Not in the middle of all these people. She drank in his stormy demeanor. The deadly intent raging in his ebony eyes. *Then again, maybe he would.*

He started walking. She followed, conscious of more than a few curious looks following them. "You're making a scene."

"Does it look like I *care*?"

Uh-oh. Her heartbeat sped up into an insistent staccato as he skirted the house and took a pathway through the forest down to the water. The farther they got from the crowds milling around the property in loose-knit groups, the worse her trepidation became. Finally, they reached the boathouse, which looked more like a full-fledged house to her with its clapboard walls and big windows. An outside lamp at the front sent a swath of light spilling across the water.

"Harrison—"

He pulled to a stop on the dock and let go of her hand. "You are *not* interested in him. You told me that."

"No, I'm not," she fired back, trying not to be intimidated by his aggressive stance, feet spread apart. "But I thought it might be nice to have a little honesty between us. You are jealous, Harrison. You are feeling things for me you won't admit, not even to yourself."

His eyes flashed. "Oh, I've admitted them to myself. I'm way past that."

She blinked. Swallowed hard as he took the two steps between them and glared down at her with the full force of his fury. "You want honesty, Frankie? Yes, I hate the look of you with Coburn because I know you don't want him. You want me. And he is a *predator.*"

"He is not. He was just having some fun with you."

His jaw hardened until his face took on the consistency of granite. "You think that's a good idea?"

She shook her head. "No, I—" She put her palms to her temples. "It wasn't."

"You don't want me, Frankie." He kept going as if he hadn't heard her. "Tell yourself that. You want a tidy little relationship with a nice guy who will treat you well, give you the requisite two-point-one kids and take you to church on Sunday." He shook his head. "That's not me."

"I never said that." A funny feeling unfurled inside of her. "Why don't you tell me what these feelings are you're having before I make a decision like that?"

He shook his head, a wary look in his eyes. "It won't accomplish anything. I have nothing to offer you."

Frustration burned through her. "I swear I will turn around, go back up there and find one of those eligible men and flirt like crazy if you don't start talking."

His throat convulsed. For a minute she thought he was going to walk away. Then he took the last step toward her, his gaze dark and tormented. "You make me want things I can't have."

"Like what?" She was hypnotized by the confusion in his gaze. The honesty.

He cupped her jaw in his hands. "You make me want you. *Need* you. Crave to be with you. I don't do relationships. That's why I walked away. Not because I don't have feelings for you."

Having his hands on her again felt *so* good. She wanted to purr into him like a cat. Her gaze held on to his. "Maybe you don't know what you're capable of."

"Even if I was," he said harshly, "you are goodness, Frankie. I am the darkness. I would only drag you down there with me."

She moved closer because she was melting inside. "I can handle myself quite nicely, Harrison. I did the other night."

He looked down, as if he was studying the heat drawing them together. "You can't handle my life as it is. With Leonid. Siberius. I could be walking into a whole other playground in a few weeks, one I'm *sure* you couldn't handle."

A presidential campaign. Rumors had been swirling all night about it. Everyone expected him to do it. But she didn't care about that. She cared about the man.

She swallowed hard. "That night at your penthouse… I've never felt like that about anyone. I've never had that kind of a connection with anyone. It was—" She shook her head, stumbling over the words. "My feelings are scaring the heck out of me, too, Harrison. I don't know how to handle them. But I won't deny them." Her gaze clung to his. "You said I make you feel alive…*you* make *me* feel alive."

His gaze darkened. He was silent for a long moment, long enough for her to hear her heart beating in her ears. "You'd be smart to walk away. If I don't break your heart now, I will later."

"You don't know that." She stepped closer until the heat of their bodies melded into one another. "There are no sure things in life. You can't insulate yourself against pain. It's impossible."

She thought she might see a flicker of awareness in his eyes. That she was right. That he'd been locking his feelings away for far too long. Her heart thrummed in her chest as he brought his mouth down to brush against the corner of hers. "There are far better bets than to take a chance on me. I'm not going to lie."

"I don't think so." Her soul reached out for his. "Let yourself go. Follow your instincts. I'll jump if you will."

He murmured something unintelligible against her mouth. Sparks flew between them, their bodies too close, too aware of their wanting not to seize it. Take it. His mouth shifted to cover hers more fully. She moved into him, like water finding a path again. After the uncertainty of this past week, she wanted comfort. She wanted to know she was right.

He kissed her hard, his mouth hungry, lacking in finesse. She had pushed him out of his comfort zone. His hands moved restlessly down to shape her breasts, the curve of her thighs through the silky material of her dress. "You look so good in this," he muttered when they came up for air. "I almost knocked Coburn senseless."

She smiled against his mouth. "He was provoking a reaction."

"He succeeded." The hand that shaped her hips pulled her hard against him. His arousal lay between them, potent and ready. Frankie gasped. "Harrison."

He grabbed her hand and walked toward the boathouse. She tugged on his fingers in a halfhearted protest. "Not here."

"You wanted me to go with my instincts. Live with it." He pulled open the door and tugged her through it. The interior of the boathouse was dimly lit, wooden seating surrounding the empty slip where the water slapped against the boards.

"Isn't everyone supposed to be down here soon for the fireworks?"

He backed her up against the wall, his gaze dark and

dangerous. "We have a good twenty, twenty-five minutes. More than enough time."

Fire raged in her belly, a forbidden, excited pull tugging at her insides. *Really? He was really going to do this?*

"People saw us leave." She attempted a last-ditch effort at sanity.

He pushed the straps of her dress off her shoulder and put his mouth to the rounded curve. "This would not be the biggest scandal in history. Trust me."

That didn't actually convince her, but his hands peeling her dress to her waist distracted her enough that she forgot all about it. She was braless beneath it, the style making undergarments impossible. His rough rumble of approval reverberated through her head. He cupped both breasts in his big hands, bending his head to capture one in his mouth. His lips and tongue played with the hard peak until it was distended and throbbing. Until she was aching inside. Then he switched his attention to the other.

His palms made a foray under her dress and pushed it up her thighs. Her silk panties were a mere wisp of fabric under his heated gaze. He left them on and dropped to his knees. His rough command to hold her dress up was all that proceeded the hot possession of his mouth on her.

Oh, dear God.

Frankie leaned back against the wall, hands clutching her dress, eyes closing at the long, lush strokes of his tongue. Her fingertips dug into the wood on either side of her. His strokes moved deeper, came harder. The only sounds in the boathouse were her breath coming in quick pants now and the water slapping against the wood.

"Harrison."

He nudged her legs farther apart with his elbows. His big hands held her thighs wide as he took her apart with deep, urgent strokes. With a tunnel-visioned focus on the throbbing center of her that shattered her completely. Her moan as she came was so loud in the echoing space, it froze her in place.

What if someone had heard?

Harrison rose. His expression was beyond caring, beyond anything except his end goal. He picked her up, braced her back against the wall and released himself, his strength, the bulging muscles of his biceps as held her in place, a massive turn-on. He moved the fabric of her panties aside and notched his erection into her hot, aching flesh. A low groan tore from his throat. "Please tell me you're protected." She nodded, not sure she would have stopped him even if she hadn't been. She was that far gone.

He buried his face in her neck. Took her with a forceful thrust that stole her breath. She pressed her head against the wall. "God—that's…"

He withdrew and thrust into her again. And again. She dug her nails into his biceps and held on. She wanted everything he had to give her, every piece of the wildness, because it gave her hope he could let go. That he would give in to the magic that was them.

Strain wrote its way across his face as he increased the pace, chasing his pleasure. Frankie brought his mouth down to hers. "Now."

He took more of her weight in his hands, ground his hips against her until his movement set her flesh on fire. She writhed against him, helped him reach the spot she needed. He didn't stop until she groaned in his mouth and sensation ripped her apart again. Then he tightened his hands around her hips and found his release. Hot, hard and uncontrollable, his orgasm sent a flood of warmth through her. It was the most complete she'd ever felt in her life.

It was long seconds later, minutes maybe, before either of them moved. Harrison let her feet slide to the floor, his face buried in her neck. A thin layer of perspiration blanketed his brow. Her heart struggled to find its normal rhythm.

Voices outside ripped them out of their stupor. Her heart crashed against her chest. *Oh, my God.*

Harrison recovered before she did, pushing her dress down over her hips and sliding the straps over her shoulders. "Fix your hair," he muttered, reaching down to make himself decent. She moved her hands up to smooth it but so many curls had escaped, there was no way she was getting it back the way it had been.

The voices got louder. They were directly outside. She threw Harrison a panicked glance. "I can't fix it."

He ran the back of his hand over his brow. "Forget about it. It looks windswept."

He straightened his jacket and reached for her hand. "The side door. We can slip into the crowd."

They exited the door, emerging into the cool night air to find most of the party had moved down to the shore for the fireworks. Any hope she had of stealthily merging into it was crushed by the appearance of Evelyn Grant, a frown on her face, Coburn directly behind her. Coburn's eyes went to her hair, which was always perfectly in place. Widened. Then it traveled to Harrison who looked utterly cool and collected. Coburn's gaze dropped lower. Frankie's followed. *Oh, dear lord, no.* Harrison had a dirt smudge on the knees of his trousers. *Both knees.*

Coburn turned away. Frankie saw his shoulders shaking. Evelyn Grant waved a finger at her son. "Honestly, Harrison. The only thing I asked you to do was round up people for the fireworks."

He lifted a shoulder. "Frankie hadn't seen the view. Apologies, forgot all about the time."

Evelyn's mouth pursed. "Can you at least ask them to start?"

Harrison kept her by his side as he walked over and

gave the instructions to the crew. He tucked her in front
of him, arms around her, as the fireworks exploded across
the sky, crackling into a starburst of red, blue and white,
the brilliant stars falling down around them. She leaned
back in his arms. The dazzling display felt like a stunning
new beginning of something. Harrison lowered his mouth
to her ear. "We made better ones."

The display went on for almost twenty minutes. The
Grants had spared no expenses tonight in this marquee
party of the year that celebrated the end of summer. She
glanced around at the crowd. Looked directly into a pair
of big blue eyes on their left that looked utterly shattered.
Cecily.

There are far better bets than to take a chance on me.

A knot formed in her stomach. Was she being incredibly foolish taking this jump? Utterly naive? Because that
sandbox Harrison had talked about…it wasn't her world.
This wasn't her world. She could easily get eaten alive.

His arms tightened around her. She nestled into him as
the fireworks came to an end. Faith required a whole lot
more determination than that type of thinking.

She stood by Harrison's side as he and Evelyn waved
the guests off in the driveway. If his mother thought her
presence there of interest, she didn't show it.

When most of them had left, except for a few stragglers
still partying on the dock with Coburn, Harrison clasped
her hand in his and they walked toward the house.

The big mansion was silent after the noise of the crowd.
They climbed the stairs to the guest rooms, but Harrison
didn't stop there; he kept going up the next flight toward
his.

"Tongues are wagging," she said quietly as they walked
down the hallway toward his suite.

He twisted the knob on the door to his room, opened it
and pushed it in with his palm. "Let them."

The room was impressive and warm with its elaborately carved wood fireplace and king-size bed. Harrison came up behind her, put his lips to the nape of her neck and sent shivers down her spine. She leaned back into the heat of his mouth, into the storm they had unleashed. Because she was most certainly in love with him. And she'd been brought up to trust her heart. She only hoped she could trust Harrison with hers.

CHAPTER TWELVE

ROCKY ADJUSTED TO his former home far more easily than Frankie did. He'd resumed his habit of swimming lazy circles to show off his magnificent burnt orange color, his elegant snout pitched in her direction to make sure she was watching, as well as his more frequent naps on the enticing, mossy crystalwort that lined the bottom of the tank.

He'd also clearly taken a cue from the more relaxed demeanor of his owner. Frankie was happy to be back with Coburn where she knew exactly what was expected of her. The work was challenging and satisfying and if there was a part of her that missed the excitement of working with a man whose multiple facets posed a different challenge every minute of the day, she had more than enough of that to contend with in her burgeoning relationship with Harrison outside the office.

He was complex and intense in everything he did, including the bedroom, where he was demonstrating just how passionate and multifaceted a relationship between a man and a woman could be.

Heat drew a curtain across her cheeks. That was where she liked him the most: in bed, where he couldn't get enough of her; where he showed how he felt without the words he couldn't seem to find. He had awakened a side of her she hadn't known existed. A confident, vital part of her that suggested maybe she wasn't so ordinary as she'd always suspected; that maybe she was much more than that. And although she still wasn't completely sure he wouldn't break her heart, she grew more confident every day in what they had. And one day at a time was how she'd promised herself she was going to play this.

Rocky swam another lazy circle in front of her, his beady eyes staring at her. "Yes, you're gorgeous," she told him, shutting her computer down as Coburn put on his coat. "But now I must leave you for a glass of wine and a good book."

"Not with my brother tonight?" Coburn came to stand by her desk.

She shook her head. "He's having dinner with Tom Dennison."

His mouth lifted in a wry tilt. "A full-court press, I'd say. They want him badly."

But did Harrison want them? It was a question she kept asking herself as she got to know the enigmatic man better and better—one she hadn't been able to answer yet. "Far more illustrious company than I," she offered drily, pulling her bottom drawer open and reaching for her bag as the elevator chimed its arrival.

Coburn's eyes moved past her to the elevators. "I think you underestimate your appeal."

She turned. Registered the dark and dangerous presence of the man who was her lover striding toward them. Her pulse shifted into overdrive. Although his eyes had the bruised look of someone who had slept even less than usual of late, undoubtedly due to his showdown with Anton Markovic next week, and the frown that marred his brow made him look forbidding, he was still the most handsome, electric man she'd ever encountered.

The trace of suspicion in his ebony eyes as his gaze flicked to Coburn's position beside her desk sent a warm, heated feeling through her. She liked him jealous. It made him just that little bit vulnerable she needed to get inside.

"H," Coburn greeted him. "Dennison stand you up?"

"I canceled."

Canceled?

Coburn straightened, moving away from her desk and the line of fire. "I'm taking it you aren't here for me. In which case, I'm going to get going. I'm meeting friends."

Harrison nodded. "I'll see you tomorrow morning."

Frankie caught the flash of emotion that passed through Coburn's eyes as he said good-night to her. He wished Harrison would confide in him. The distance between the brothers was becoming so clear to her. She waited until Coburn had stepped on the elevator and left before turning her gaze on the man who'd taken his place. "You know it hurts him when you shut him out like that."

He wrapped his fingers around her wrist and brought her to her feet. "Coburn and I are complicated. Don't get in the middle."

But she knew he didn't bite now, despite his reputation. "Was it always like this?"

His ebony eyes flattened into a matte black. "No. We were close once." He slid an arm around her waist and pulled her close. "We took two different paths. It's years of history. Stop digging."

"Okay," she murmured, suddenly feeling out of breath as he bent his head toward her. "There are security cameras here...remember?"

He kissed her anyway, the heat of his mouth burning through any resistance she had. She curled her fingers into the lapels of his jacket and kissed him back. He didn't stop until she was fully distracted, a deep sigh pulling from her throat.

"Have dinner with me tonight," he murmured huskily against her lips. "Unless you have plans..."

"With a pizza box and a book." She pulled back and studied his weary face. "Why did you cancel?'

A grimace stretched his lips. "I can't think when they're all over me."

Yet he'd chosen her to be with. Heat radiated from her chest, spilling into every part of her. "Yes," she accepted, running her fingers over the taut skin of his cheek. "If you agree to order pizza."

He produced the pizza and a bottle of Chianti, an easier battle than it might have been given it was Elisa's night out and his food snob tendencies couldn't take over.

"You know," she murmured when they'd demolished the pizza on the sofa in the showpiece of a living room, "this decor doesn't suit you at all. It doesn't say anything about who you are."

His lips curved. "I could tell you hated it from the minute you walked in."

"I don't hate it. I think it looks like an art gallery, not a home."

"It's supposed to be an investment."

"Do you plan to live here for a while?"

"Unless plans change."

Unless he ended up in Washington...

He waved an elegant hand around the space. "What would you do, then, with it?"

She gave the open-concept, stark room a critical once-over. "I would add some of that color you love, maybe a gray blue for the walls. Carpets to give it warmth, definitely. And maybe some exotic accents."

He cradled the big wineglass in his palm. "You think that's me?"

"I think it's complex like you are... You aren't cold like this, Harrison. You're layered, you have great depth of feeling when you allow yourself to experience it."

Surprisingly, he didn't back away from the assessment.

His face was lost in thought as he sat there in a rare still moment. "I can't afford to be emotional right now," he said finally, his dark lashes coming down to veil his expression. "Too many things depend on me being level-headed."

"My father always taught me to go with my gut," she countered. "He said the rest will come if you start with what's in your heart."

He lifted his ebony gaze to her. "What if your heart's conflicted?"

Her heart squeezed at the admission. "You need to find out why."

He rested his head against the sofa and stared over at the beautiful Chagalls, both of them in place now. Frankie swallowed hard. "Where is the push for politics coming from? Is it your dream or is it your father's unfinished one?"

He blinked as if he couldn't believe she'd said it. Her hands tightened around the glass, her pulse speeding up. The moment hung in the air between them like an irreversible stepping stone to an intimacy he didn't know how to traverse. Then he sat back and swirled the wine in his glass, his eyes on the ruby-red liquid. "It's both," he said finally. "Politics is in my blood. In my family's blood... My grandfather was a congressman, my father would have been governor had he not taken his own life. You talked about giving back to the community on our flight to London... *I* want to do that. There are so many things I want to change, things I know I *can* change. But am I the right man for the job? This isn't about what I want. It's about what this nation needs."

Frankie felt the overwhelming sense of responsibility coming off him in waves. She couldn't imagine how he felt, but she could try. "I think the country needs hope and vision," she said quietly. "People need someone to believe in. I've seen you lead, Harrison. You've turned a company that was on the verge of disappearing into one of the most powerful in the world. You know how to do this."

He was silent for a long time then. His eyes when he looked at her held that same darkness she'd seen that night she'd rescued him from himself. "Sometimes too great an ambition can destroy a man."

He's worried about becoming his father. Suddenly she understood what had been eating him that night, what had been eating him ever since he'd signed that contract with Leonid. *I am the darkness,* he'd said to her that night in Long Island, *I would only drag you down there with me.* He was afraid of being consumed by the same disease that had taken his father. And who wouldn't be?

She put her wineglass down, got up and settled herself on his lap, knees on either side of his muscular thighs. "You are not your father," she said, cupping his jaw in her hands. "He was sick. You are strong."

His body tautened beneath her like a big cat ready to spring free, but she held his gaze firm in hers. He inhaled deeply, then exhaled, a warm rush of air brushing her cheeks. "He fell apart the night before he announced he was running for governor. I think after what Markovic did, the pressure was too much for him."

Her heart ripped to shreds. "He was on the verge of losing everything. It's understandable. *You*, you are walking into this having conquered. That's a whole different thing. I've watched you do superhuman things. You do what the analysts say can't be done."

His mouth twisted. "Expectations are a bitch, Frankie."

She smiled at that. "I know all about expectations. I'd be running Masserias right now if I'd done what everyone expected of me, and it wouldn't have been the right road for me." She fanned her fingers over his beautiful, tense face, so full of everyone's expectations but his own.

"Figure out if this is *your* dream. If it is, make it happen. If it isn't, walk away."

He captured her fingers in his own, the depth of emotion in his dark eyes making her heart turn over. "I'm done lecturing," she murmured, tugging her fingers away to start undoing the top buttons of his shirt. "Should we discuss the weather now?"

A new emotion joined the ones spiraling through his conflicted gaze. *Desire.* "Only if the forecast involves all my clothes coming off," he said roughly.

"Eventually." She dropped her mouth to his hard, muscular torso as her fingers worked the last buttons free. He shrugged out of the shirt and sat back. Her fingers went for his belt, sliding it free from the buckle with industrious swiftness. Her lips and tongue made a foray down over the hard wall of his abdomen. The muscles beneath her lips contracted with every inch she traveled, until she reached the waistband of his pants. His breath was faster now, his anticipation firing her blood.

"*Hell*, Frankie…"

She undid his pants. Slid the zipper down and released him. He was all hers, this powerful man, and she wanted all of him. *All* of him.

His intake of breath drowned out the blood pounding against her eardrums. She had never done this for him, had never done it for any man. But he was too intoxicating to resist. She bent her head and took him into her mouth.

He cursed and arched beneath her. She refused to let him hurry her, taking her time exploring every musky, potent inch of him that knew how to give her such pleasure. He was big and beautiful and she was shocked at how much she loved touching him like this. Tasting him. It was such a potent turn-on it threw her right into the melee with him. When his hands bit into her biceps and he lifted her from him to rid himself of his pants and then her of her underwear, she didn't protest. Her dress bunched in his hands, he brought her down on him in a joining so fierce, so complete, it stole the breath from her lungs.

"Was that enough of the angel for you?" she murmured when she finally recovered enough to meet his dark, bottomless gaze.

His eyes glittered back at her. "*You* are my angel," he murmured in a gritty voice that made her heart swell. "I love how you rescue me."

She closed her eyes as his hands on her hips guided her down over him again. "You make me crazy," he told her on a half groan. "I can't make this last."

She dug her fingers into the hard muscle of his shoulders to tell him he didn't need to. His fingers clutched her hips in an almost painful grip as he took over the rhythm, driving them both to a powerful climax. It rocked her, taking her apart from the inside.

Shivers snaked through her as he stroked his hand down her spine, his touch on her skin a sensory overload. Emotional overload.

He carried her to bed and made love to her again. Frankie thought that finally, in the aftermath, her head on his shoulder, she had cracked the beast. That she had found what it was inside of him that had needed to be found. *Healed*. For if she hadn't, she had most certainly just sealed her own fate.

CHAPTER THIRTEEN

THE NIGHT BEFORE Harrison confronted Anton Markovic in Washington, Frankie's family invited them to dinner at Masserias. She was concerned, he knew, about how tunnel-visioned he'd become in the past few days and was attempting to distract him. It was a good attempt, her boisterous clan loud and entertaining, but tomorrow was weighing heavily on his mind.

He should have felt settled, confident, with everything in place. He'd brought Siberius under the Grant fold with what looked as if it was going to be minimal intervention from the regulators. He knew exactly when and where he would intercept Markovic. But still the rush wasn't coming. The bloodthirsty urge to tear the Russian from limb to limb that had fueled so much of his adult life hadn't materialized. Instead grim determination defined him. A desire to put a chapter of his life to rest. To avenge the honor of his family. His father.

Frankie's clear, perfect laughter filled the table. Salvatore was teasing her about her taste in music. The happiness written across her face touched something deep inside him. He knew it was she who was changing him. She who was balancing out his extreme emotions. Every day he spent with her he felt more whole, more at peace. She was more than he ever could have anticipated having.

Wanting. He couldn't feel numb with Frankie in his life. She surrounded him in emotion. But having lived so long without it, it was as if he was in the middle of a maze with untold treasures at the end of it, but if he took a wrong turn, it could all end in disaster.

Terrifying.

He took a sip of his Chianti. Forced himself out of his introspection. The Masserias were a fascinating clan to watch as they interacted. He'd never seen such a close-knit unit. Even though all of them were different, from psychologist Federica, with her dry wit and calm demeanor, to Salvatore, Frankie's favorite, with his aggressive, acerbic personality, the depth of caring between the siblings was obvious. They may not all be close—indeed Frankie had filled him in on the tensions between the different factions—but he had the feeling they would all do anything for one another if push came to shove. The bonds were that strong.

A pang seared his heart. He had never had this, a family unit to support him. Not even before his father had gotten sick. It had all been about building the empire for Clifford Grant. About ascending in society. Family had taken a backseat. But he did have Coburn, whom he'd once been close with, the only warmth that had existed within the cold, formal Grant family walls. But his brother's attempt to party and daredevil his way out of his grief had pushed them far apart, a gap that had grown with every year.

He took another sip of his wine and set the glass down. It was eating away at him, had been ever since Frankie had offered that observation about them that night at the office. He hadn't realized until then how much he had missed his brother.

His gaze collided with Vanni Masseria's across the table. Frankie's father was watching him with a probing look: measured, assessing. As if he was weighing his in-

tentions. Harrison met his gaze evenly. It was easy to see
where Frankie got her charm and wisdom. Vanni was a
charismatic, self-made man who knew himself. Who knew
the world from the perspective of a successful man who'd
worked hard and prospered just like Harrison's own father
had. He also knew Harrison was older than his daughter
and much more worldly. That if he put himself in a presidential race it would thrust Frankie into a cutthroat, very
public world she'd never known.

Harrison shifted his gaze to Frankie, wondering how
she would handle the pressure of being a politician's wife.
Would she carry that effortless charm and composure of
hers to the role as easily as she'd slipped into his life and
found her way inside him? Inside his heart? Or would it
drown her? *Would being a Grant make her lose herself?*

He didn't blame Vanni Masseria for being wary. He
was, too.

Frankie followed Salvatore into the kitchen, dishes in hand.
Her brother set his stack of plates down, turned and leaned
against the counter. "I like him."

A weight lifted off her chest. She set her pile of plates
down beside his, realizing how nervous she'd been bringing Harrison here for this impromptu dinner. Things were
still so new between them, and her family meant everything to her. If they hadn't liked Harrison it would have
put her in a turmoil.

Even more so than she was in right now.

Salvatore eyed her, his guarded expression suggesting
that *liking* wasn't all that mattered. "You know what you're
doing? He's a bit out of your league, Franks."

She chewed on her lip. Why was it every time she was
around her family, she ended up feeling insecure? Unsure
of herself? She loved them, adored Salvatore, but she hated

the feeling she got in the pit of her stomach when they questioned her actions.

She lifted her gaze to her brother's. "Apparently he isn't since we're together."

He shook his head. "You know it's true. Two weeks ago you're telling me he's escorting you to a party but he's not your date. Now you look like you're head over heels for him." He rubbed a hand over his goatee. "You work for him, Franks. He's a Grant. A hard, ruthless businessman. It's worth keeping your head is all."

"I'm happy with him."

"That doesn't change the fact he knows his way around a woman." His eyes lost their aggressive edge. "Look, I am happy for you, sis, I am. Nobody likes to see the sparkle in your eyes more than I do and he gives that to you. But I'm a man. I can see when a guy's got a lot going on in his head. Just take it slow."

Harrison did have a lot going on in his head. He was flying to Washington tomorrow to confront Anton Markovic. It made her sick thinking about him coming face-to-face with the man who'd destroyed his father.

"It's complicated," she told Salvatore.

He grimaced. "That's a fancy word we men use to define *unsure*."

The knot tying itself in her stomach grew tighter. And larger, as she and Harrison said their goodbyes and drove to the penthouse. He was quiet in the car, quiet as they rode the elevator up to the swish, elegant lobby. She could feel the tension gripping him, watched him retreat into his head. She'd wanted to be here for him tonight because she'd known he'd be keyed up about Markovic. And he was.

"They liked you," she murmured when he rose, went into the kitchen and came back with coffee for him and herbal tea for her.

He gave her one of those blank looks he'd been wearing all evening. "I liked them, too. You're lucky to have them."

Something he didn't have. She curled her fingers into his thigh. "What's wrong?"

He looked down at her fingers. "I'm just distracted. A million things on my mind."

"Are you sure you still want to do this?"

His gaze lifted to hers, fiery now. "No sermons, Frankie, I can't take it tonight."

She bit her lip. Tomorrow he was going to take his revenge on a man who had stolen his father from him. It wasn't the answer to his anger, but he couldn't see it.

"It won't bring him back." She dug her fingertips deeper into his thigh. "Nothing is going to bring your father back, Harrison. Nothing is going to right the wrongs Anton Markovic did. The only way forward is for you to forgive him. To move on and honor your father like you have been."

"Forgive?" His mouth flattened into a straight line, his thigh tensing beneath her fingers. "That's what your *new-age advice* would tell me to do? What exactly is that supposed to accomplish, Frankie? I'm supposed to become at peace with the world by doing it?"

She winced, but his anger no longer had the power to silence her. She knew he didn't bite. "You're making it sound too simplistic. You have to let go to move on. Hatred is toxic. Hatred is what gives you these black moods. They aren't going to go away unless you get rid of the poison behind them."

He stood up. His gaze was beyond lethal as he pinned it on her. "*He* is the poison. *He* is the toxicity. *He* needs to be broken."

"And then what? You destroy him and take everything? You think you are going to miraculously feel better because you did the same thing to another man that was done to your father? Did you ever think that he might have a family, too? That he might have children who will be as broken as you and Coburn if you do this? If you take away their livelihood?"

He lifted a shoulder. "He should have thought about that before he played so cavalierly with other people's lives. You can bet if he conducts business this way we were not the only victims. There are others, and I want him gone so he can never do it again."

She couldn't argue with that point. Juliana had told her what an evil man Anton Markovic was. But evil had nothing to do with this. In taking Markovic down, Harrison would give his own soul away. He was halfway there now.

"Ask yourself," she said quietly, "if you can handle the guilt when it's all over. Ask yourself if it's worth it. Because I saw your face after Leonid signed that contract. You are an honorable man. But you won't consider yourself that if you do this tomorrow."

An expression she'd never seen before passed over his face. Shock that she'd said it? Anger that she'd dared? Fear she was right? Her blood raced in her veins, making her feel light-headed. She had gone too far. But she'd never have forgiven herself for not saying it before it was too late.

He turned and walked away from her, out onto the terrace. She gave him a few minutes, then followed. He stood looking at the smoky skyline of Manhattan, shrouded on a smoggy, summer night.

"You think you know me," he rasped when he sensed her behind him. "But you don't. You think everyone is good like you are, but they aren't. You're an anomaly in a world where greed and selfishness rule."

She moved beside him so she could see him, see the torment on his face. Her blood pounded hard in her ears, warning her to stop, warning her she'd already pushed him far enough and he was letting her in slowly but surely. But she couldn't because he needed to hear this.

JENNIFER HAYWARD   175

"You tell yourself that because it's easier to believe. Because it's easier than admitting the beautiful human man that you are inside that cast-iron exterior. I can't watch you do it, Harrison. I am beyond that."

"Then leave." His harsh words hit her like a slap in the face. She braved his anger and put a hand on his arm. He shook it off, his eyes cold. "It was a mistake thinking this could ever work, Frankie. I told you that in Long Island, but you wouldn't listen."

"Harrison—"

"Leave." His gaze tangled with hers, like polished stone. "I don't want you here."

Her heart fell apart. She should be used to how brutally cold he could be but it didn't prepare her for the way she shattered, tiny fragments of herself raining down over her until she felt as though nothing was left. Only a searing pain that seemed to transcend her body.

He had the ability to make her feel everything. And nothing.

Her hands shook as she pushed her hair out of her face and looked up at him. "You're right. I don't know you, then. Because I thought you were more than this."

She turned and left the penthouse, tears threatening to penetrate her numbness. She'd thought she'd been getting through to him, that something was clicking in that closed-off brain of his. But she'd been wrong. The beast could wallow in his self-imposed misery. She was done.

CHAPTER FOURTEEN

THE PRIVATE CLUB in the heart of downtown Washington where Anton Markovic was meeting a senior government official had been described as "the closest thing to the unofficial heart of the city's intellectual elite" that existed. Housed in an elegant Louis XVI–style townhome on Embassy Row that had once been a private residence, it had been the meeting place of presidents, Supreme Court justices and Nobel Prize winners over its history.

It was the type of place that, should he run for office, would define Harrison's life. He entered the wood-paneled library with its refined decor and elaborately carved fireplaces and took a seat near the windows. You could almost *feel* the backroom conversations that had shaped a nation. It was that steeped in tradition. *Prestige.* He felt underdressed even in a suit.

Locating his target sitting across from a salt-and-pepper-haired bureaucrat near one of the fireplaces, he took the opportunity to study him. Anton Markovic was in his late fifties, graying at the temples, handsome by anyone's standards. But it was the cruel edge to his mouth that drew his eye. The knowledge of how much devastation he had wreaked with a calculated move to save a failing empire.

His body went ice-cold, as if it had been February, not

the last sweltering days of August in a town built on a swamp.

He was not letting him walk out of here intact.

Markovic gave him an absentminded look, as if he half recognized him but was too wrapped up in his conversation to pursue the thought. Harrison sat down in a chair beside the fireplace and waited. It was another half hour before the two men stood, shook hands and walked toward the stairwell. Harrison unfolded himself from the chair, intercepted them at the door and held his hand out to Markovic. "Harrison Grant."

The bureaucrat looked intrigued to see him there. A wary glitter appeared in the Russian's eyes. "A pleasure," he said, shaking his hand.

Bile pooled in the back of his throat at the touch of the other man's hand. He brought a practiced, easy smile to his lips. "Could I steal you for a drink? I had something I wanted to discuss with you."

The suspicion in the Russian's eyes intensified. "I'm afraid I have dinner plans."

"Ten minutes." Harrison made it rude not to accept. *You'll want to hear what I have to say,* his eyes told the Russian. *And not in front of your companion.*

Markovic nodded and said his goodbyes to the bureaucrat. The Russian waited until the other man had cleared the landing and was walking down the lower stairs before he spoke.

"I had the feeling our paths might cross someday."

The way he said it in an almost casual tone, the complete disregard for the tragedies he'd instigated, brought Harrison's breath to a halt in his throat. The man was a monster. Without feeling or soul. He'd heard he was this way but it was something else to see it in the flesh.

"Sit down." He bit out the words before he clawed the other man's eyes from his face.

The Russian sat, his expression still that cool, controlled mask. "So?"

Harrison sat down. His disbelief overrode the speech he had rehearsed in his head hundreds of times. "You don't care, do you? What you did to my family?"

Markovic's eyes flashed a frigid blue. "I didn't kill your father, Grant, he did. Things happen in business... He could have done what you did—moved past his mistake and rebuilt. Instead he was weak."

Harrison's rage descended to a bone-deep level that scared even him. It made it almost impossible to move, to speak. "You don't feel the slightest bit of remorse," he managed finally, "for what you did?"

The Russian shrugged. "I'm sorry you lost your father. I'm sorry he had a disease. But he chose to make the deal."

"*He didn't know what deal he was making.* What you did was amoral and illegal. Today you would be prosecuted."

"Good thing yesterday isn't today. And we all know I suffered, too, Grant. I failed. I lost everything. I was going through my own personal hell."

"Get ready to go through it again."

Markovic's eyes flickered. "How do you figure that?"

Harrison leaned forward and rested his forearms on his thighs. "I've bought up every single one of your key suppliers. Through offshore entities, subsidiaries, friends. When I flick a switch tomorrow morning, you will be missing one part, then another. Production will be delayed, then delayed some more. Until one morning you wake up and your entire operations have ground to a halt and you are *paralyzed*. And then I don't care if you feel remorse. I only want you to experience the *hell*."

The Russian's face went gray. "It's a global economy, Grant. There are any number of other suppliers I can turn to."

Satisfaction lanced through the numbness blanketing

Harrison. "Try it." He nodded in the direction the bureaucrat had taken. "But I advise you do it before you sign your contract. You might find yourself *unable to deliver.*"

A sick realization spread across Markovic's face. Harrison stood up. His skin felt too tight to be in the presence of such ugliness any longer.

Not one more second would he let this man rule his life.

"Enjoy your dinner."

He walked past the tapestries, the paintings three presidents had considered while they had changed a nation. Away from his past. Toward his future. And wondered why it still didn't feel right.

A whisper-quick flight later, the Grant jet deposited him back in Mahattan just before eight. Standing on his terrace with a whiskey in his hand, watching the lights from the skyscrapers cast the city in a glow of prosperity versus the history of Washington, New York seemed a lifetime away from Anton Markovic. From his past.

Someday you're going to realize that cold heart of yours has left you alone in this big empty world, H. And when you do, nobody is going to care anymore.

The empty feeling in his gut so perfectly matched Coburn's prediction it was like a knife twisting a particularly painful path through him. How his brother and Frankie had both known so clearly that vengeance was never going to give him the satisfaction he craved made him wonder how well he knew himself. Avenging his father's honor was the phantom, the mirage that had kept him going all these years, but when it came down to it, Markovic had been right: his father had been sick; the Russian had not been responsible for his death.

The whiskey burned as he took a long slug of it, but not enough to ease the self-knowledge that seared him. He had wanted to hate Anton Markovic rather than acknowledge the disease that had ravaged his all-powerful father. Because if it could happen to a force like Clifford Grant, it could happen to him.

He cradled the crystal tumbler in his palm and watched the light bounce off its carefully crafted edges. Funnily enough, what was hurting him most wasn't the past, which he knew now he needed to let go. It was Frankie. He was afraid he was that cold-hearted monster Coburn had painted who had driven away the woman he loved for good.

That he loved her his heart had acknowledged weeks ago. His head had simply refused to follow. The question now was whether he deserved a chance at happiness. Was he *enough* to make her happy? Would the darkness continue to move away with her in his life or would he destroy her?

His fingers tightened around the glass. He wished he had a crystal ball that would give him the answers he needed. He was terrified instead that putting his heart on the line was the only thing that might save him.

Something latent but still alive stirred inside him. He had to try.

CHAPTER FIFTEEN

"I'M BANKING ON the fact you have beer in this bachelor pad."

If Coburn found it odd that his older brother, who rarely drank beer and even more infrequently dropped by for a chat on a Wednesday evening, was standing on his doorstep, he refrained from commenting. His expression, though, as he stepped back and Harrison walked in, was wry. "You're going to have to let me finish up. Carole is here."

"Finish up?" Coburn glanced in the direction of the bedroom. Harrison ran a hand through his hair. "Good God, Coburn." He turned around and headed for the door, but his brother stopped him with a hand on his arm.

"She's getting dressed. She has an early yoga class. Stay."

Harrison went to the kitchen, grabbed two beers from the fridge and headed for the patio. He tipped the beer back and drank a long swallow while he watched what appeared to be a raucous party on the patio opposite Coburn's in the trendy Chelsea neighborhood.

His brother came out, pulling a T-shirt over his head. Harrison handed him his beer and nodded toward the door. "You know you're going to have to get rid of *that*."

"When I'm seventy, maybe yes."

"Sooner than that. That type will get far too attached to the idea of bedding a CEO. Of being *the one* beside all that power."

The bottle stopped halfway to Coburn's mouth. "You're going to run."

He nodded. "You think you can take over without driving us into the ground?"

His brother put the bottle down. Iron determination filled his face. "You know I can."

"I do." Harrison tilted the bottle at him. "The press conference is tomorrow to announce my candidacy. I'd like you to be there with me."

To any other brother, the command would have sounded arrogant. But Coburn knew what it took for him to ask for support. His brother's eyes glimmered with an emotion he hadn't seen him exhibit in a very long time. "I'll be there."

They drank in silence for a while. An ache filled Harrison's chest. He'd missed this. More than he'd known. "How do you even sleep with that racket going on?"

"I don't...much." Coburn turned to him, resting his hip against the railing. "What happened with Markovic?"

"I took away enough of his suppliers to hamstring him but not kill him. He's going to spend the rest of his days remembering what he did." He shrugged. "Or maybe not. The man has no conscience."

"Why didn't you do it? Why didn't you annihilate him?"

He lifted a shoulder. "Because you were right. Doing that isn't going to bring back our father. And at the end of the day, the fact is, Dad was sick. Markovic didn't kill him, the disease did."

"And you are better than that." His brother's look was pointed. "I was waiting for you to realize that."

"Someone else helped me realize it."

Coburn's eyes sharpened on him. "She's miserable, H. You did a number on her."

His heart turned over in his chest. "I know. I plan to fix it." He just wasn't at all sure what the outcome would be. It had his insides tied into a knot.

They talked about tomorrow. About the future of Grant and their roles in it. Harrison would stay as involved as he could for as long as he could. But the CEO role was Coburn's—permanently. If politics didn't work out for him, well, they'd cross that bridge when they came to it.

Coburn walked him to the door. His eyes were full of life. Full of challenge. He'd been needing it for a long time.

Harrison did something he hadn't done in as long as he could remember. He wrapped his arm around his brother and hugged him hard. Then he walked out into the night before Coburn saw the tears stinging his eyes.

Masserias was buzzing on a Thursday night with every table in the restaurant taken and the overflow spilling to the bar. The patrons were in a universally upbeat mood, it seemed, enjoying good food and wine before the weekend.

Frankie took the order from her table, walked to the computer and punched it in. She was grateful for the infusion of energy, had volunteered to take this shift from a sick waitress to help her parents out, because if she stayed at home and moped for another night she was going to turn into a permanent case of pathetic.

"Well, I'll be damned." Her father's voice carried to her from the bar where he was mixing drinks with Salvatore. The bemused tone in his voice drew her eye.

"What?"

He pointed at the TV mounted on the wall to one side of the bar. Frankie skimmed the headline. *Harrison Grant to join the presidential race as an independent candidate.*

She moved closer, her heart stirring to life in her chest. Her father turned up the volume so the announcer's voice could be heard over the crowd. *"Grant confirmed the long-*

anticipated news today that he will run as an independent candidate for president. The CEO, whose grandfather was a congressman and whose father took his life the night before his announcement he would run for Governor, of New York, gave an emotional speech about the financial well-being of a nation he described as 'struggling to find its identity.'"

Her heart, which hadn't come close to repairing itself, swelled with an ache so painful it winded her. A clip of Harrison at the podium filled the screen. "I believe in a nation where things can be better. Where we can all believe in who we are again, where we can have faith in the principles this country was founded on. And that starts with the people." He paused, his gaze trained on the cameras. "Someone recently reminded me of the goodness of people—how every decision we make impacts not only us but the people around us. And that goodness—that caring for each other—is what the fabric of this nation was built on. It's what we need to go forward. My vision is about putting the people first again with a back-to-basics fiscal policy shaped by the principles that created this country. We all want to contribute. We all want to make our mark. And we will."

Her heart throbbed in her chest. The announcer wound up the story and invited a panel of guests to discuss how Harrison's entry into the race would affect the dynamics. Her father slapped his hand on his thigh. "Well, I'll be damned," he said again. "He's actually going to do it."

Her eyes were burning. She turned away from the screen, but not before a tear slipped from her eye and eagle-eyed Salvatore saw it. A dark look spread across his face. He knew how badly she was hurting.

"Franks—"

She waved him off. "I need that Bellini."

An order was up for her in the kitchen. She waited

for the chef to set the last plate on the counter. *Someone recently reminded me of the goodness of people*. He'd been talking about her, she was sure of it. Tears streamed down her face. She grabbed a napkin from the counter and mopped them up. She was so happy for him and so utterly miserable at the same time. She wanted him to heal, wanted him to move on, but she wanted it to be with her. She might only be twenty-three but she knew when someone was your soul mate. The problem was, you couldn't make someone love you. She knew that, too.

She composed herself, picked up the plates and headed back into the dining room to deliver them. Table served, she went to collect her Bellini at the bar. It was waiting for her. She slid it onto her tray.

"Aww, hell."

"What?" She turned in the direction of Salvatore's scowl. A dark-haired male clad in a black trench coat was talking to her mother. He was too arresting, too handsome to ignore. He looked exactly like he had the night he'd walked into the office and all hell had broken loose. Except he had a bouquet of red roses in his hands.

Her mind lost all conscious thought, including the fact she was holding a tray. The Bellini hit the floor with a loud crash that had all eyes on her.

It was the roses that did her in.

Her gaze locked with Harrison's. He looked so serious, so intent it stopped her heart in her chest. You could hear a pin drop in the room as eyes moved from her to the man who'd just been on TV. The need to escape the attention, *to do something*, sent her to her knees. She right-sided the tray and started picking up the pieces of glass. Salvatore dropped to his knees beside her and brushed her hands away. "Forget about the goddamned glass," he muttered. "Go talk to him before I kill him."

She got to her feet. Most of the crowd in the restaurant

had gone back to their conversations, but there were a few who were too interested in the news of the day to want to miss a thing. Her pulse fluttered wildly in her throat as Harrison headed toward her.

He stopped in front of her, his gaze eating her up. "My effect on you hasn't seemed to change."

She swallowed hard, pride kicking in. "Don't be so sure about that."

"Oh, I *am*."

Heat invaded every cell of her body, thrumming through her veins. "Congratulations on your announcement," she said stiffly. "You have everybody in a flutter."

He reached out and ran a finger down her cheek. "The only one I'm interested in having in a flutter is you."

She flinched away from his touch. "You ended that on Monday or have you forgotten?"

His gaze darkened. "Do you think we can have this conversation in private?"

"No." She shook her head, too hurt, too unwilling to go there with him when he'd made it clear they were over. "You can't push me away then expect me to fall into your arms again when it's convenient for you, Harrison."

"That's not what this is."

"Then what is it? You told me it was never going to work. Don't come to me on some high then break my heart again. I can't take it."

"I've changed." His voice vibrated with emotion. "*You've* changed me, Frankie. You've made me see how wrong my thinking was. How capable I am of feeling."

Her heart started to melt despite herself. He saw it, pressed his advantage. "Give me another chance. I promise I deserve it."

She crossed her arms over her chest, holding in the surge of hope that took ahold of her. "Why should I? What's going to be different this time?"

"Me." He stepped closer until he was occupying her personal space. Every cell in her body reacted to him. Begged her for him. His eyes were the deepest black she'd ever seen them, except now, she realized, they were clear, without a shadow of doubt in them.

"My head has been so messed up. I've had so many decisions to make, so many ghosts to put to rest, I couldn't think straight. But you," he said, reaching for her hand, "you are the only thing that's been right."

She shook her head, wanting him so badly it hurt. "I can't be a part of your endless circle of revenge. It will eventually tear you apart and me along with it."

"It won't. I'm stepping down as Grant CEO. But I have gained the board's assurance that Siberius will remain a separate company. Leonid's wish will be fulfilled."

Something shifted inside her. She had dangled that possibility in front of him that night in bed, hoping he would see he had alternatives. But he had shut her down so completely she had given up hope. "And Markovic? What did you do with him?"

His jaw hardened. "I put him on notice that if his behavior ever gets beyond my tolerance, I will take him apart. Meanwhile, I left him enough lifelines to stay alive."

"Why?" She could hardly get the word past the lump in her throat.

"Because one tragedy does not equal another. Of all the crimes Anton Markovic has perpetrated on my family, killing my father was not one of them. My father was teetering on the edge. I needed someone to blame instead of facing my own rage. My sadness."

She saw for the first time the vulnerable edge to his decisive, steely exterior. It was there just behind the blazing confidence in his eyes, that soft amber light she'd discovered in the office that day. She swallowed hard as she digested it all. The things he'd done had proved beyond words that he did want to move beyond the darkness. That he meant what he was saying.

But she had no idea where to start. He did. He put the roses on the bar, took her hand and dragged her from the room.

"Harrison…"

"Where?" he growled. "I've had enough of an audience today."

"The staff room," she offered weakly, pointing at a door past the kitchen. He opened the door, but there was someone in there. Cursing, he found the next available door and yanked it open. It was a supply closet. He pulled her in and closed the door behind them. She was too full of emotion to do anything but stand there, back against the wall in the tiny space as he curled a hand around her nape and brought her to him. The glitter in his eyes made her insides contract. "I love you, Francesca Masseria. Your goodness, your passion, everything about you. You have healed a broken part of me I thought forever lost."

Her heart leaped into her mouth and stayed there. She couldn't get a word past her lips. Not one.

"The next year is going to be crazy," he continued, "and I know it's a lot to ask of you, but I want you by my side during this. Actually," he amended, "that's not true. I want you by my side always."

Her breath escaped in a long, harsh expenditure of air. "Harrison—"

He let go of her, reached inside his jacket and came out with a box. Her brain went haywire. "You aren't going to—"

"Propose in a supply closet?" He dropped to his knee. "I tried to go somewhere private."

"Yes, but—"

He flipped the box open. A sparkling sapphire winked back at her, surrounded by the most perfect row of white fire. She stared at it. Stared at the powerful, ruthless man at her feet who'd just declared his intentions to run this country.

"Marry me," he murmured. "Be my anchor in this storm because I need you there."

Could she be a Grant? Could she be a politician's wife? He was asking her to take a leap just like she had asked him that night in Long Island. And although the idea scared the hell out of her, her heart wouldn't let her do anything but follow it.

"The answer is yes," she said softly, "if you promise me that when things get dark, you won't shut me out. You will talk to me."

She thought she saw moisture build at the corner of his eyes. It made hot tears gather in hers. "I promise," he said, his voice steady and sure.

She stuck out her hand. Held her breath as he slid the sapphire on her ring finger. Because it had to fit. *They* fit perfectly. She was strong where he was weak and he was all-powerful in the spaces between.

It fit.

He rose to his feet. She threw herself into his arms, every bit of pent-up emotion bursting out of her as he anchored her against him and kissed her. Sure and never-ending it was heaven.

His palms moved lower on her hips, settled her more intimately against him. Frankie drew in a breath at the white-hot heat that consumed her at his blatant arousal. "We are *not* doing this here."

"No," he murmured against her lips, "I value my life. But I need five more minutes."

When way more than five minutes had passed, they emerged from the closet, clothes intact, a bloom in Frankie's cheeks that made Salvatore's face darken when they walked back into the dining room. She held up her left hand and the glare faded. "You are a lucky man, Grant. By the skin of your teeth."

Her brother's face relaxed into a beaming smile as he stepped forward and shook Harrison's hand. The bubbly came out and the night devolved into a restaurant-wide celebration, on the house.

Her father and Harrison spent the night talking politics while her mother plied her about dress choices between customers. But Frankie wasn't ready to think about any of that. She wanted to savor every minute of the weight of Harrison's ring on her finger.

She heard her father say something about hosting a rally here at the restaurant for Harrison's campaign. "We've created a monster," she said rolling her eyes.

Salvatore gave their father an amused look. "He should have run a long time ago. Let him live vicariously through your fiancé."

Fiancé. The glow lasted all the way home to Harrison's penthouse. In the elevator where they almost lost control completely, then in the bedroom where her *fiancé* disposed of her clothes so fast her head spun. She lay back on the bed, watching him as he prowled toward her. "Maybe you should come work for me on my campaign. I can live out my fantasy. *Daily...*"

She dug her fingers in his hair as he pressed a kiss to her throat. "I have never dropped a drink in my life until tonight. I'm done working for you, Harrison. You have me entirely on edge."

His gaze glittered. "Actually," he murmured, "I completely agree. The only place I want you off balance is here. *Under me.*"

She could offer her full cooperation on that. Her insides contracted with the need to have him after a week full of misery. But it was his clear, unclouded gaze that touched her the deepest. In that moment, she knew she could do it.

She could be a Grant, and maybe, if the stars aligned, she could be a president's wife. Because she was the woman who'd conquered the heart of the beast. The woman who'd helped heal him.

She smiled and closed her eyes as he dragged her down into the tempest with him. They'd said it was impossible. What did they know?

* * * * *

*If you enjoyed this book,
look out for the next installment of*
THE TENACIOUS TYCOONS
Coming October 2015

HARLEQUIN

Presents®

Get ready to be dazzled by the amazing
Sharon Kendrick's
most recent story, filled with power,
temptation and excitement!

THE RUTHLESS GREEK'S RETURN

July 2015

CEO Loukas Sarantos's most recent
procurement means he can finally take revenge on
Jessica Cartwright—the *only* woman to ever walk away
from him. But Loukas soon begins to realize Jessica may
be the most precious jewel in his possession...

Stay Connected:
www.Harlequin.com
www.IHeartPresents.com
f /HarlequinBooks
🐦 @HarlequinBooks
P /HarlequinBooks

HP13354R